HELEN GRIFFITHS

The Mysterious
Appearance of Agnes

Illustrated by Victor Ambrus

HOLIDAY HOUSE · NEW YORK

Library of Congress Cataloging in Publication Data

Griffiths, Helen.
    The mysterious appearance of Agnes.

    London ed. (Hutchinson Junior Books) has title: Witch
fear.
    SUMMARY: A small child who mysteriously appears in a
remote sixteenth-century German village develops into an
emotionally disturbed mute and is accused of witchcraft.
    [1. Witchcraft—Fiction.   2. Emotional problems—
Fiction.   3. Germany—Social life and customs—Fiction]
I. Ambrus, Victor G.   II. Title.
PZ7.G8837My   [Fic]   74-21793
ISBN 0-8234-0267-3

About 1540

One

When Agnes first came to the village most people agreed that it was the work of God. It was not until several years had passed that the same people began to murmur that perhaps they had been misguided, that perhaps her appearance, as mysterious as it was unexpected, had been in fact the advent of the Devil.

The village was in a beautiful place, sheltered from the worst winter storms by the mountains that reared up steeply on every side. There was water in abundance; streams and springs and a surging river along whose bank led the only road to civilization beyond the undulant peaks. Thick pine forests gave way to oak and chestnut and beech woods on the lower flanks of the mountains, and in the valley itself the earth was black, rich and succulent.

In springtime everything was green in a dozen different shades. In late summer all the valley was golden with rye, while in the autumn – the dying time, the time when Agnes first appeared – the colours were tawny and red, burnished with the last of the year's splendour before the commencement of the snows.

Although many villages at that time were surrounded by high wooden palisades whose gates were barred at night, this was not the case here. The hundred or so dwellings, mostly of mud and wattle, extended along the valley in scattered fashion. Only the church, the public meeting house and the two taverns were solidly built and close to each other. There was a prosperous air about these and the well-stocked gardens which was reflected in the genial, robust features of the inhabitants.

The villagers knew there were other hamlets in other valleys but few of them had ever seen them with their own eyes. Travellers came along the road by the river, their ponies laden with things from the outer world, things that the villagers could not produce for themselves – salt and spices, silk and knife blades. The travellers told them how the war was progressing and how those who escaped blood and fire were brought down by the plague. They rarely came with any news that was good.

Therefore the inhabitants of that beautiful valley knew they were lucky, that God had blessed them, keeping them safe from pestilence and roving bands of mercenaries. They decked their church with utmost splendour, the women vying with each other in the freshness and originality of the flowers cultivated in their gardens, while the images of the Virgin which protected the main pathways through the fields were decked with wild flowers according to the season.

Agnes did not come along the road. She came from the forest, picking her way through the stubbled field that bordered its edge, stopping now and then to rub her nose or scratch her head, or to disentangle her dress from the stiff cut edges of the stalks. The day was dying, like the season, and already there were more shadows than light across the valley.

Josef was taking home his two milch cows when he saw her. At first he thought she was one of the village children who had strayed too far and he halted to wait for her, the cows sleepily swishing their tails and ruminating beside him. There was something about her that held his attention, something in her appearance – the sun burning in her hair and across her ruddy face, her nonchalance, her unhurried pace – which kept him rooted there. He told himself it was his duty to scold her and escort her back to her parents but, deep inside himself, he knew it was something more than that.

('It was as if I couldn't move, as if I had to wait for her,' he was to remember years later, when they said she was a witch.)

When she was close enough for him to see her face clearly he knew she was a stranger. Her eyes were blue, her hair was flaxen, her cheeks were rosy beneath their dirt. She was about three years old. She looked just like many another village toddler but she was the daughter of no one there.

He looked beyond her to the dark shadows among the close-growing trees, but no one followed her, no one waited for her. She was a small child alone, who had come from the forest with bits of twigs and bracken stuck to her hair and skirt, fine scratches on her face and earth under her fingernails.

When she was only a few feet away from Josef she stopped and looked at him – at least, it seemed as though she looked at him, although the expression in her eyes was quite unlike any he had seen before. It was as if she looked without seeing.

'Who are you? Where do you come from? What's your name?' Josef bent towards her as he spoke, stretching out his free hand.

She stood still but made no answer. She was neither pleased nor afraid. She did not look back when he picked her up – there was obviously no one to look for, no one she belonged to – and she said nothing and hardly stirred all the way to the priest's house, which was where Josef took her because he did not know what else he should do.

*

'What's your name, child? Where is your mother? Where do you come from? Have you no father or mother?' And again, 'What's your name?'

In the gloomy, candlelit room the questions were put at first gently and then with some exasperation by the priest and several neighbours who had come quickly at the sight of Josef with a child in his arms instead of just Josef with two cows. Each one thought he or she knew best how to coax the child into speech. One caressed the grubby cheek, another proffered a russety apple, the priest dangled his rosary before her, wondering if the beads or the crucifix would attract her attention. Like Josef, he was puzzled by her expression.

Agnes pushed into her mouth the bread that was offered to her and greedily drank down a bowlful of fresh milk, obviously hungry. She took the apple and sniffed it before biting into it, but she did not speak.

'Perhaps she's deaf,' suggested someone.

'Perhaps she's dumb,' said another.

'Perhaps she's an idiot,' voiced a third.

'Perhaps she prefers not to speak.' This was from Josef who had remained aloof from the interrogation and exclamation until now.

The priest looked at him sharply, realizing that he too had sensed something strange about her which had gone unnoticed by the rest, but before he could take him up on his words there was a scandalous interruption. A woman in worn grey home-spun burst through the door, followed closely by a man who vainly sought to detain her.

'Where is she? Where is she?' screamed the newcomer, pushing people aside. 'They told me there was a child, a little girl . . .'

She stopped short at the sight of the small figure sitting on the table, apple in hand, jaws working imperturbably, then she flung herself upon her and dragged her into her arms.

'She's mine! Mine!' she cried, glaring ferociously from one to another, expecting the child to be snatched away and unaware of the amazement in their expressions. She turned on her husband with the same wild glance. 'She's mine, I tell you. Mine.'

The husband tried to calm her. 'Wife, wife . . .' but she was aware of nothing beyond the flaxen-haired child clutched close to her breast.

'Good woman,' said the priest, motioning the others to make way for him. 'Calm yourself. She's not your daughter, as well you know. Josef has just found her and brought her here.'

'Agnes!' The name was a wail of desperation.

'Agnes is dead and buried these three years,' the priest firmly reminded her. 'This child is another, or would you have it that the good Lord rejected her and sent her back to walk the earth again?'

'Agnes,' repeated the woman, but now her voice had lost its fierceness. With a gesture of defeated despair she allowed her husband to take the child and hand her back to the priest who placed her on the table again, where she went on eating her apple, unaware of the woman's devouring gaze.

'She's done nothing but pray for a daughter ever since Agnes died,' the husband awkwardly explained. 'It's become an obsession. We've had no more children. She was the only one. You know how she has prayed, Father,' he appealed to the priest. 'You know that I've prayed too.'

The priest nodded thoughtfully.

'And my prayers have been answered at last,' broke in the woman, excitement showing in her eyes again.

Her arms went out towards the child, though her husband restrained her.

'He has sent her, sent her to me. "Ask and ye shall be given." Isn't that what you have told us Father? I've begged on my knees on every Holy Day, I've prostrated myself before the crucifix on countless occasions, I've accepted every penance with joy, knowing that one day the Mother of God would have mercy on me, that She would remember my misery, recalling Her own, and give me back my daughter Agnes.'

It was impossible to ignore her. Everyone knew of her agony at her daughter's death and her growing misery and frustration when no other child was born to her. No one had the courage to say that the child should not be given into her care after the priest's next words.

'The child shall be yours then, on the condition that should someone come to claim her you will surrender her without complaint. A man shall be sent to all the villages to seek information as to her parentage. If nothing comes of these enquiries the child will be yours. She shall be baptized –'

'Her name is Agnes,' broke in the woman.

The priest looked at her husband and was satisfied with the plea of comprehension he saw there.

'As you will. Agnes then.'

With unbelieving eagerness she gathered the child in her arms once more and hurried away home. As soon as she was gone a general discussion broke out as to where the child could have come from. Only Josef had nothing to say and he also went away before the priest could question him.

Two

Klaus and Wilhemina had been married for ten years before their one and only child was born to them and since her death, three years later, there had been no whisper of hope or joy in their stunted lives. For the last five years Wilhemina had prayed in every way she knew but the anguish of her loss had never left her heart. Her husband's clumsy efforts at consolation fell on barren ground and, although his own pain at the child's loss had since faded into an occasionally recalled memory, he was bitter with a sense of injustice.

Without changing its exterior aspect, their very dwelling had lost its homeliness and grown like those who lived within, dry and silent. There was one big, windowless room with a fireplace where they ate and slept, with its few bits of roughly hewn furniture, and a smaller room beside which served as a stable for their few animals.

Klaus had been a strong, frank-eyed youth when he married Wilhemina, handsome enough in his way for all the unmarried girls to blush and flutter a little at the sight of him. Wilhemina had never been more than plain, but the warmth in her gay grey eyes had been sufficient to capture the young man's heart in spite of her long, thin nose and colourless hair. After the first hopeful years the warmth of expression had faded, not to return until the birth of little Agnes when, for the first time, it seemed that happiness and fulfilment brought a serene beauty to her features and Klaus again remembered why he had once loved her.

The sweetness of those three years while she lived was just sufficient to blight the rest of their existence at her death. After that there was no purpose in life at all for either of them until a lost and nameless child, looking so much like their own little Agnes, was given into their keeping.

*

Agnes made no reaction when they brought her to their home. Klaus set about stirring up a blaze in the fireplace while Wilhemina sat the child on her lap and crooned over her. Agnes did not listen to her words but stared about, looking up at the dusty thatch beyond the rafters, along which mice scuffled at nighttime, and then watching the flicker of light which Klaus was coaxing from the wood. There was no telling what her expression meant. If she thought or felt anything it was well disguised.

Wilhemina was so contented to have the child on her knees, in her arms, warm against her breast, that she did not notice her strangeness. Love overflowed from the withered heart while her fingers picked the burrs and bits of leaves from the untidy hair, and forgotten cradle songs came to her lips. But Klaus, with his back turned and unable to see her face, felt the gaze that moved from place to place slowly and without remark, and there was a feeling of fear within him. Fear because the way the child had come was very strange; fear because no one knew anything of her background; fear because he had brought her into his home for his wife to love and because she was the most unchildlike child he had ever witnessed.

Eventually Wilhemina put her to sleep in the cot that had been their daughter's and which had stood empty at the foot of their own bed for so long. She tossed and turned and uttered whimpering sounds, but she did not wake, not even when the woman anxiously stroked her brow. They watched her by the light of the fire, wondering who and what she was, but not yet daring to discuss her.

In the morning she was awake before they were. Klaus

found her in the stable, sitting on the manger at the cow's head, stroking it between the eyes. For a moment the cow turned to look at Klaus, then pushed its head close to Agnes again for more attention. Agnes did not even look at him and Klaus did not know what to say to her. The night before he had determined to treat her as a daughter, for his wife's sake; had planned how he would pick her up, hug her perhaps, and ask her what she had dreamt that night; but he found himself wordless when at last she gazed at him, her expression wide and deep and loveless.

'Come and fetch her,' he called to his wife after a few moments, unable to touch her in spite of his resolution, and Wilhemina took her back to the living room to wash and dress her.

'How's my darling this morning? Are you hungry? What bad dreams made you whimper so? Do you like the cow? Today I'm going to give you some new clothes and after breakfast we must go to church. My little Agnes, my sweet little girl! What scratches you have on your face and hands! Did you fall in the forest? Were you lost?'

She talked and talked. Klaus could hear her as he milked the cow but Agnes said nothing. She allowed the woman to do as she would, accepting the brown, home-spun dress which had belonged to the former child and the bowl of body-warm milk Klaus brought in for her, and as soon as Wilhemina left her alone she ran back to the stable to sit with the cow again.

Klaus looked at his wife. 'Has she said anything? Has she made any sound at all?'

Wilhemina shook her head, but added swiftly, 'But she will. I know she will. She feels strange. That's all it is. When she's used to us it will be different. We must be patient, that's all.'

'Where is she from? That's what I would like to know. Perhaps her parents died of the plague. Perhaps she'll bring it to the whole village. Perhaps we ought not to have her here.'

'It's more than likely that her home was destroyed by soldiers or bandits. Who knows what terrible things she may have seen? Perhaps that's why she doesn't speak.'

They discovered that she was not deaf. Sharp sounds startled her and she was keenly aware of the birds that squabbled in the eaves of the house. If she could hear those slight, whispery sounds she could not possibly be deaf.

The days went by and each morning Wilhemina woke with the same fear, that this might be the day when some news would come from another village of a lost child. The days drew into weeks and Wilhemina's fear was even more acute because by now the priest's messenger must have reached the town which was said to be many days' journey away, but when the messenger returned he had nothing to tell them.

'No one seems to have lost a child. There has been no new sickness, no looting soldiers, no strangers. No one knows where she can have come from.'

But if Wilhemina's heart was gladdened and relieved, Klaus was silently troubled. He had been certain that someone would claim her, someone would know who she was, and he wondered if she or her family had some bad history which was being deliberately concealed. He himself, unknown to his wife, had gone several times to the forest in search of some clue. He found a scrap of her dress caught on a holly bush, where red berries already gleamed, but that was all. He had hoped to find a body – her dead mother, perhaps – but the only sign confirmed what he already knew, that Agnes herself had passed that way. Whether accompanied or alone, it seemed that he would never know.

Klaus had grown no closer to her over the weeks. He had tried to feel some warmth for her, the natural warmth of friendship towards a small child, but even this would not come to him. He could talk to any child in the village, fashion a toy out of wood if they asked for it, and he had particularly wanted to love this child for Wilhemina's sake. But whenever Agnes gazed at him he found himself speechless, and cold inside, and had to turn away.

He observed his wife and realized that she, too, could make no headway with her. The difference between them was that she felt so much love for Agnes that the child's indifference to all her attentions went unnoticed. Wilhemina overflowed with love, with the desire to give, to cherish, and it was enough that Agnes did not exactly reject her in order to be satisfied.

Closely watching her, it seemed to Klaus that Agnes was more like some small animal, speechless but understanding, needing no affection, having none to give. She was obedient, but she did not belong to them and did not even care to try to reach their hearts. Wilhemina would sing her songs and tell her stories and Agnes would sit patiently until the songs and stories had ended. Then she would get up and run off, as if she knew that she had done her duty, and Klaus could see that none of his wife's love had touched her in the slightest. This hurt him cruelly, although he did not know how to say so.

When he tried to express his observations and opinions Wilhemina would not listen and even accused him of jealousy.

'You're making a fool of yourself over that child,' he shouted at her. 'Can't you see that I'm right, or don't you want to admit it? She isn't Agnes, not our Agnes, and she never will be. God knows I was only too willing to take her in for your sake, but now I wish I hadn't. You do everything for her and, as far as she's concerned, you hardly even exist.'

'I love her and that's all I care. When she gets older she'll be different. You'll see. We must only be patient.'

Klaus snorted disbelievingly.

'And even if she doesn't change I'll still love her.'

'She'll break your heart, that's what she will do. She's hard. She feels nothing. You'll never make her love you however much you try.'

*

Winter came. The mountains were covered with snow and all roads and paths were blocked. No one could leave the village now, or enter it, until the spring thaw. The forest was dark and silent, the trees heavily garlanded with whiteness which had swallowed the meadows and most of the landmarks and through which the wooden village houses stuck out starkly. The water was frozen and icicles gleamed in the sunlight.

Inside the house it was warm. Klaus had piled up a big stock of logs to feed the fire, while the animals in the stable let out a musky heat which permeated the whole building. On the farthest side of the room Wilhemina had laid out the pears and apples from her garden which were to last all winter. There was bracken and straw for the animals and sacks of flour for bread, ground from the summer's rye. It was in this corner, dark and warm, that Agnes most liked to be when it was too cold to be outside. She would huddle up in the straw and, amid the perfume of apples and sweet bracken, fall asleep.

Three

Several years went by and Agnes grew into a slender child of introverted expression; lost-looking, it was said. By now everyone in the village was used to her. They all knew she never spoke and they pitied Klaus and Wilhemina for having adopted her. Most people said she was an idiot and the children laughed at her when they saw her. Their parents warned them to have nothing to do with her and the most notice they would take of her, if they happened to see her alone, was to throw stones and insults after her.

Wilhemina had taken her to church every day, convinced that a second miracle would occur, that the child she had been given would develop the power of speech, and then she had fallen back on to older customs, deeper superstitions, in her longing for Agnes to be like everyone else.

One day, when Klaus had gone off to his labour, she wrapped a shawl round her head and shoulders and hurried in the opposite direction, beyond the orchards, where a narrow stream trickled down towards the river. It was a deserted spot, for as long as people could remember this shallow rivulet, appearing from a cave-like opening in the earth, had been associated with spirits and strange occurrences. No one would allow their animals to drink there, for it was said they would immediately fall sick and die, and children were commanded to keep away from its banks.

Around the dark hole from which the water trickled

were seven flat stones. No one knew how they came to be there in that semicircular position, the water passing on either side of the central stone. All about them the grass grew thick and lush, mingled with rushes and wild flowers, but a sombre darkness was cast over the whole by a wide-spreading yew tree whose heavy branches touched the water itself. It was the biggest of a grove, dominating the stream and meadow with sinister majesty.

It was here that Wilhemina came and, after cautiously assuring herself that no one was about, she drew out the small jug of milk she had hidden within the folds of her shawl and the shallow dish into which she poured its contents. She placed the dish on the central stone and prayed with all her heart for Agnes to be cured of her strangeness, promising to refill the dish as often as she was able.

Thus had her mother and grandmother prayed, with an offering of fresh milk either to please or appease the spirits. It was a thing no one spoke of, except in whispers and with great secrecy, but many of the women returned to the invisible spirits of the woods and water when their prayers to the Virgin had gone unheeded. Klaus had forbidden his wife to continue this practice, when once he discovered her praying this way for the child. He had no belief in such nonsense but knew that it could be dangerous for a woman to be caught praying to invisible powers unconnected with the Holy Trinity.

So now she went in secret and took a lock of the child's fair hair, which she placed beside the dish of milk, believing that in this way the spirits would know to which child she referred, and when she returned a week later the dish was clean and the lock of hair had disappeared.

In spite of her frequent visits to the secret place, in spite of her constant prayers both to the old gods and the new, Agnes remained dumb and indifferent. Klaus even went so far as to part with a few of his precious coins when a travelling apothecary appeared in the village one day but, in spite of his knowledge and the various tests he made which proved there was no physical defect to account for her silence, he was unable to enlighten the peasant any further.

Her relationship with Klaus and Wilhemina had hardly altered since the first day they had brought her to their home. She felt a certain trust for the woman, showing it only in small ways as when occasionally she would thrust some wilting bluebells into her hands or leave a stone of unusual shape or markings in a place where Wilhemina would be sure to find it.

While she was small she had never strayed far from the house. In good weather she was always outside but she did not play as other children played. Wilhemina had made her a rag doll but she did not care for it at all and when she was not just staring into space she would crumble earth between her fingers or sit for a long time stroking a smooth stone. This last irritated Klaus beyond all reasoning and when he saw her at it he would slap the stone from her hands, then turn away before he caught the uncomprehending gaze she shot at him.

Now and again Klaus would be overcome by a feeling of shame or remorse for neglecting her. Then he would reach out to her, wanting to say something to her, but she always withdrew sharply, like a frightened animal, and then he would be angry, with himself for having believed that the effort was worthwhile and with her for having proved to him that it was not. How could he possibly find a way of understanding that speechless, almost emotionless, child that fate – God or the Devil, he still did not know which – had thrust upon them?

As for Wilhemina, by the time Agnes was eight the

21

raging fire of frustrated motherhood which had caused her to confuse the identity of the little foundling with that of her own dead daughter had dissolved into mute misery at having failed to gain her love. All that remained was a sense of duty, a fear of being ridiculed by the village wives if, after her vehement protestations, she were to admit that she had failed. She dared not even voice her secret feelings to the priest and she believed that only she was aware of them, she and the sprites to whom she had confessed her insufficiency and begged for power to make Agnes love her.

She tried to hide her growing apathy by acts of ever greater devotion and she never ceased fluttering about the child, talking to her, asking questions which would never be answered, answering for her to disguise the silence, until at times Klaus could bear her jabber no longer and shouted for silence.

The first time Agnes came home with bruises on her arms and blood on her face from the stones the boys had thrown at her, Wilhemina was filled with a sense of shame. A sudden wish that the stones had killed her gripped her with horror and she thrust the thought into the deepest part of her, wondering how such wickedness could come into her mind. Because of her secret thought she treated Agnes with greater gentleness, kissing the cuts and bruises after carefully cleaning them, and really he did not know whether she loved her or not.

'Why don't we send her away?' Klaus once suggested when Agnes was out of hearing.

Her startled look made him realize that the idea was not new to her but her answer came sharply. 'How could you even think such a thing?'

'Serving girls are always needed at the hall. She wouldn't be ill-treated there. She would be fed and given somewhere to sleep.'

'But what could she do?'

'Look after the geese or the pigs. She doesn't need to be able to speak for that.'

Wilhemina was silent and Klaus thought she would agree.

'We should never have brought her here,' he went on, thinking to animate her, to make her capitulation easier. 'Of course, we couldn't know then what she would be like, but even you have to admit that the day we brought her here was the day a curse came upon us.'

'Klaus!' His wife crossed herself rapidly.

'It's true. Don't try to deny it. We thought she would bring us happiness but she's brought us only shame and misery. We've done our best for her. We have nothing to be ashamed of. It's time now for someone else to take her in hand.'

'You would turn her out as if she were a dog that had failed us as a guardian, a cow that threw sickly calves or a hen that had stopped laying? We didn't take her in for the happiness we expected her to bring us.'

'Sometimes I wonder why we did take her in,' the man brooded, looking older and greyer than his wife had ever noticed before. 'Sometimes I wonder if we had any choice in the matter.'

'What do you mean? What are you trying to say?' There was fear in Wilhemina's eyes.

'You know what some of our neighbours are saying. You've heard them, perhaps more than I have. You know why the boys stone her and the girls run away at the sight of her. They say there's a curse on her. They say she's bewitched. They say she's a changeling.'

'No. No. I'll never believe that.'

'Our own child died,' went on Klaus remorselessly, hardly hearing her exclamation, 'and we are denied another until this – this – ' he searched for a word and almost spat as he went on, 'this creature appears mysteriously, in a way that no one has been able to explain. You go into a fever over her, insist that she must be yours, call her Agnes in a fit of craziness, can hardly even recognize her as not your own flesh and blood. Perhaps I can understand your feelings,' he mused, 'but why should I have agreed to your madness? I knew from the beginning there was something strange about her. I knew from the beginning that it would be useless, so why didn't I have the strength there and then to oppose your wishes?'

He looked squarely at Wilhemina and said, 'I tell you, wife, we are being used by her and it's got to stop.'

At this moment Agnes appeared. Whether she had overheard their conversation or not, whether she had understood it anyway, they could not tell, but their own sense of guilt made it seem that she looked at them with a wisdom greater than their own. Wilhemina was suddenly afraid and pulled her into her arms to cuddle her.

'She's our daughter. I love her. I want her to stay with us,' she cried.

Tears fell into the child's fair hair but Agnes stood stiffly heedless.

Four

Klaus tried to make Agnes useful in the fields. He had several strips of arable land where he grew oats and barley, potatoes and other vegetables. In springtime flocks of birds would settle among the furrows, intent on devouring the seed that was spread over the newly ploughed earth. The flapping rags of the scarecrow were ineffective and Klaus sent Agnes out early each morning to run up and down the furrows to keep the birds away.

He told her to throw stones and showed her how to set traps for them, because a few blackbirds or skylarks for the cooking pot were always welcome. She spent the whole day in the fields, and was expected to return home at the setting of the sun, when the birds also retired, and each evening she returned empty-handed.

Puzzled, Klaus decided one day to watch her without her knowledge and he was amazed to see that the birds had no fear of her whatsoever. She sat on the ground and crumbled her bread for them, scattering it in a circle about her, and was quite motionless while the birds hopped closer and closer. A robin went so far as to perch on her knee. He flew off when the wood pigeons arrived, for whom Agnes spread still more of the bread that Wilhemina had given her, but the sight of these robbers gorging themselves with such satisfaction was too much for Klaus.

He sprang up from his hiding place and, shouting with fury, startled all the birds into flight. In his rage he dragged Agnes to her feet then knocked her to the ground with his blows, swearing that he would beat some sense into her if she refused to understand in any other way. She did not even cry out and her petrified silence effectively curtailed his rage.

He never touched her again, neither did he send her back to the fields. He did not know what to do with her. Even if he sent her to gather wood, as likely as not she would come back empty-handed. In the end he decided to leave her to her fancies, in this way making it plain to his wife that he would be no more responsible for her. He did not turn her out of his home, as he had once suggested, but he took as much notice of her as if she were a dog come to shelter there.

Wilhemina cared for her as always, with a sense of duty that was sometimes enlightened by a longing to wring some expression of fondness from the child, but she saw that it was hopeless. As the months went by Agnes seemed to grow further and further apart from her. While she was very small there had been some signs of attachment, kindling new hope in the woman's heart, but by the time she was ten it seemed to her that Agnes regarded her with the same indifference with which she had always regarded Klaus.

Sometimes Wilhemina would see her gazing up at the moon whose light reflecting in the pensive face enhanced the distant look that was always with her. The woman did not know whether she felt fear or tenderness towards her in those moments. A feeling would catch at her heart, filling it with a kind of pain. Once she gently called, 'Agnes', and smoothed her rough hand down the long fair hair, but not by the slightest movement did the child show any awareness of her.

She spent most of the day out of doors, coming and going as she pleased. Klaus took no interest in her actions and Wilhemina did not know how to control them. She grew as wild and elusive as the small animals that attracted her. It was as if her muteness served as a bridge towards her understanding of them and a barrier to her ever understanding her own kind, from whom she was so different.

One day the priest came to enquire of her. She had been absent from the church for a long time. Wilhemina no longer took her there. She had taken her several times to the secret place but had even lost faith in the woodland sprites. Both Klaus and his wife tried to explain but broke off, not knowing how to express themselves. In the end the man said, 'Stay and have supper with us, Father. When she comes you will see for yourself how she has become and that will be better than any words of mine.'

The priest waited until nightfall and was beginning to grow impatient. All three people sat round the oak table, their empty platters before them, watching the door, from one moment to the other expecting it to be pushed open. At last the priest rose, reaching for his hat, saying with a sigh that he had other business to attend to and would return another day. Then, in her usual unself-conscious way, Agnes slipped through the half-open door and reached for her bowl which was in its place next to Wilhemina.

As far as the priest could see it was as if none of the three watchers existed. She went towards the table as if she were alone in the room, registering no surprise at the unexpected guest, no flicker of warmth, and was about to go off with her bowl when the priest detained her, grasping her arm with firm, if gentle fingers.

'Agnes!' he exclaimed. 'Don't you recognize me? Don't you remember me? It's so long since you went to mass that I've come to enquire about you.'

Earnestly he searched her face, looking for something in those strange blue eyes, but what he found caused him to withdraw his hand with involuntary abruptness. It was as if he had looked into the eyes of a dead person!

Feeling herself released, Agnes continued her way to the stable, where she sat in a corner to eat her food, watching the cows swing their tails and move their jaws.

The peasant and his wife looked at the priest anxiously.

'Her eyes are soulless!' he exclaimed, and all three crossed themselves as the words were uttered.

'I wish I knew where she came from,' said Klaus sullenly. 'I've always wanted to know.'

'We've always done our best for her,' insisted Wilhemina. 'I've loved her and cared for her but she never even sees me.'

'A dead soul,' said the priest, half to himself. To the two anxious people he said, 'You must pray. You must pray constantly. Sooner or later God will hear you.'

'But what's the matter with her?' cried Wilhemina, not satisfied with his exhortation to pray. Had she not been praying for years, while she churned the butter and baked the bread and tossed the straw in the mattress, and had she not known deep in her heart that God had not once heeded her?

'She's not deaf. She has given us a hundred proofs that her hearing is as sharp as an animal's, much sharper than ours, and yet she doesn't hear a word we say. She burned herself with the fire last winter – I can show you the scar on her leg – and yet she didn't even feel the cinder that had jumped out and stuck to her flesh. She shows us not the slightest affection and yet there's not an animal about the place that doesn't trust her. Why even –'

'Silence!' Klaus interrupted fiercely. 'You are letting your tongue run away with you.'

The priest stared severely at both of them and let his gaze linger on the woman.

'These are strange things you tell me, Wilhemina. I only wonder that I have never heard them before. I wonder that you keep so much concealed. Have you any further secrets to impart?'

'Do you call secrets the things we have lived with for years?' Klaus defended her. 'Why, we're so used to the child's behaviour that, unless called upon to talk about it, we don't even notice.'

'Everyone says she's an idiot,' went on Wilhemina in a pleading tone. 'You've heard them yourself, Father. You've seen the other children throw stones at her. You defended her once, don't you remember?'

'I defended her because I had faith in you both as her guardians to bring her up in godly ways, but all I see is that you allow her to live like an animal and have no care whatsoever for her immortal soul.'

'That's not true, Father,' Klaus answered with hardly-controlled wrath. 'We have never willingly hidden her strangeness from you. In fact, I had forgotten how she burned herself last winter until my wife mentioned it just now. We took her to church as often as we could, but tell me, Father, how do you educate the immortal soul of a child that doesn't even look at you, that never ever hears you, that drifts from place to place like a feather in the wind?'

'A good beating and a little starving often works wonders,' replied the priest tartly. 'Have you tried it, I wonder? Have you been firm enough with her?'

'I beat her once,' Klaus confessed.

'And what was the result?'

Klaus could not return the priest's demanding look. How could he confess that he was afraid of the child, that on the rare occasions that she did focus a stare upon him there was a coldness in the gaze that seemed to claw deep into his stomach?

'It didn't make her hear or see us any better,' he said at last.

'There's something very strange about that child. I must confess that once I was very much taken with her but the things you tell me tonight, and the way I see her behave – and that expression in her eyes – are giving me cause to doubt.'

'What must we do, Father?' begged Wilhemina. 'Please tell us. We'll do anything you say.'

For a while the priest was thoughtfully silent. He was equally at a loss, confronted by such strangeness, but he could not admit as much. In the end he said, 'I must give the matter some thought. Meanwhile, remember! God is not mocked.'

With this last terse comment, he bade them good night and left.

Five

The valley was usually blessed with gentle summers and Agnes's seventh summer there was no different from the rest. Spring had come with the melting of the snows which had filled the streams and the river to bursting point, while in the woods that bordered the grazing lands there were greens of every hue in the new leaves, ferns and flowers that gave shade and softness to the glades. With each passing week the skies were bluer and the clouds smaller and by the end of May the fields sown with rye were a dark and glorious green, rippling and changing with the breeze.

Agnes would sit on a hill above the fields and watch how they changed, swaying this way and that, seeming to alter colour with the wind's capricious games. She would sit for an hour thus, hardly moving, and to a watcher she would appear to be frozen or senseless until, almost imperceptibly, the still, thin body would begin to make the same gentle movements as the young spring rye . . . swaying thus and thus, compelled by the rush of the wind that bent the myriad stalks and bent her frame.

She became the rye caressed by the breeze. She was green and soft and free to sway until she was dizzy with movement and fell back to the earth, her hair covering her face, puffed by the breeze, and the sky with its few bits of clouds would swirl and sway in compass with her weightless body.

She would go into the forest beyond the fields, where the last bluebells were drooping their heavy heads to the soft damp soil, brushing the fallen white petals of the dog-roses of May. She would gather the petals and hold them gently in the palm of her hand, smoothing them with her fingertips, sniffing them, rubbing them against her cheek, and although she had not felt the cinder burn her leg, the silkiness of the wild rose petals seeped deeply into her.

Agnes had no memory of the day she had come out of the forest, barefoot and alone, but the trees and the ferns, the dark, secret places and the sun-dappled glades tempted her in a way that she instinctively understood. She wandered in silence beneath the great boughs of the oak and beech trees, her naked feet sensing the broken twigs, the dead leaves and rotting acorns of centuries of seasons. The birds were not alarmed by her, the squirrels sat and watched her, noses twitching, tails flicking. Rabbits quivered in the undergrowth but did not dart away.

She sought no friendship with the woodland animals. She had no understanding of the meaning of friendship and if the frogs and mice or birds came to her and were unafraid it was because she felt herself to be part of them, not apart from them, and they could sense this too. She projected herself into them, just as she projected herself into the water, the rye or the rose petals, and had she been able to utter any speech and someone had asked her the names of these things, she would have answered, 'Agnes'.

'Agnes' was the only human word that meant anything to her because it signified herself. Other words she understood for their surface value only and when she did not want to hear them, when she did not need them, she shut them out of her existence. 'Agnes' was the only word she could never shut out because 'Agnes' was herself.

'Agnes' she could not shut out nor escape from, but she could turn 'Agnes' into stones or flowers or frogs and feel what they felt instead of the immense loneliness of herself. 'Agnes' was only bearable when she was being something else and that was why she needed the forest and the fields which were full of things that could become 'Agnes' at her whim.

Klaus and Wilhemina tried to oblige her to be them, to feel what they felt, to act as they acted. They wished to drag her away from the only thing she understood, the only security she knew. Desolate though it was, it was security and from that inner island she refused to budge.

None of this was her own thinking, for she very rarely thought. She just felt, her mind firmly closed against any intrusion, exercising itself only in its minimum form of self-protection. Thus, when Klaus ordered her to be at the table at mealtimes she was there, because eating was a physical pleasure she would not willingly forgo.

Curling up beside the winter bracken and the sweet-smelling apples was another physical pleasure which she remembered each season. Any kind of warmth was pleasure, which was why she liked to sleep beside the cows and to be constantly near them. Pain she shut out because it was disagreeable and only the fiercest of pains would sink through to her. The cinder that scarred her leg was hardly more than a sensation for which she had no category. Thus she had not felt it in the way Wilhemina and Klaus understood.

But there were occasions when Agnes could not be dissolved into another form or feeling and then the knowledge of herself was too tremendous to be borne. Dark and scarlet shapes would tear, pincer-like, inside her, crushing and terrifying in their intensity, while at the same time everything dissolved about her, disappearing into an emptiness that overpowered her with a sense of loss, of not belonging anywhere or to anything. She was suddenly the only existent being in an utterly empty world. She would scream and scream until her throat ached, but the screams were inside her head and soul, too deep and agonizing to be uttered by a voice.

Wilhemina had sometimes seen her gripped by this inexplicable terror, which would end in a flood of tears followed by a deep sleep, but she had been too afraid to mention this to Klaus and had thrust it to the secret part of her memory. Curiously enough, it was when Agnes was occasionally overtaken by such voiceless distress that Wilhemina was most able to feel a closeness to her.

She would take the almost unconscious child onto her lap and nurse her fiercely, rocking her back and forth with a torrent of loving words. She could see the child's need of her, she could sense that all resistance was gone, and in those moments she could love her with all her heart because Agnes set up no barrier against her.

*

Agnes had no special place in the forest that she preferred to another. She would follow the chattering of a bird or the whirred scolding of a squirrel, instinctively alert to their cries. Here were no human commands to order her days and oblige her into self-recognition and therefore she could delight in the abstract pleasure of the sounds of nature; the soughing in the trees when winds tussled or changed direction, the clear sharp echo of the woodpecker at work, the cuckoo's defiant cry. In each sound was an echo of 'Agnes' and when 'Agnes' was on the outside, talking to her in a hundred different ways and voices, she was not inside herself. Like this, the nameless, personless child was happy.

One afternoon towards the end of May she was wandering beneath the full-leafed trees, her fingers brushing the ferns on either side of her, all her senses alert to the sounds of the forest, when a new cry struck through the rest. Sharp and plaintive, it reached down inside the listening child and struck painfully inside her.

It was 'Agnes' crying inside herself, hurting somehow, and suddenly all the other sounds disappeared, were gone. There was only the desperate, weary sound which ached through every nerve, demanding recognition.

She hurried towards the sound, trampling flowers and pushing through ferns, her ears sharply tuned to the direction from which it came until suddenly, unexpectedly, only a few strides ahead of her, she came upon the author of the cries – a strange, black animal, hardly as large as a rabbit, its head in a hunter's noose.

Agnes halted. Neither Klaus nor Wilhemina would have recognized the child at that moment, her intense blue eyes vividly focused upon the suffering animal. There was no soullessness in her expression now. All her being was concentrated on that other being whose voice she had recognized. It was the voice of pain and desolation, the speechless voice of 'Agnes' crying out.

*

The animal was lying on its flank amid a tangle of broken ferns which it had crushed in its struggles to release itself from the trap. The noose had only tightened itself still more and, although it was not tight enough to suffocate its victim rapidly, its inescapable hold had reduced its captive to a state of defeated terror. It had tried to tear the noose away with its claws and both chin and neck were raw and bloody. For nearly a week it had been held there. The eyes were sunken, the tongue swollen in the pain-stretched mouth, the black fur had lost its sheen and the flanks were hollow.

Unconsciously, Agnes lifted her hands to her own throat, whose muscles tightened convulsively as if it were they that felt the pressure of the noose. She sank to the ground and remained on her knees beside the exhausted animal, which no longer cried now that it was no longer alone. Its lips stretched back still farther from its fangs

35

as it produced a sharp hiss of fear, and claws flashed out
from the thin black paws. They dug into Agnes's knee
through her dress and, although she felt them, it was as
if she herself had made the action. As her hands reached
out to touch the weary body she saw 'Agnes' caught and
strangled there.

Again the claws slashed at her, this time clinging to
her arms, digging deep into the flesh. Blood began to
slide down to her wrists as she gently stroked the tense
black frame, and the claws relaxed their hold as a sense
of stillness invaded both of them in the half-sunlight of
that solitary spot from which fear and desperation had
suddenly fled.

Six

It was Josef who had set the trap, the same Josef who had seen Agnes come out of the forest and was later to declare against her. In the last few years nothing had gone well for him. Both his cows had died and his land did not produce as it should. That he was lazier than most, allowing his aches and pains to keep him from the earth when most it needed him, he himself did not recognize and he railed against misfortune when he might have been better employed railing against his own idle nature.

He lived alone in a hut dirtier than Klaus's stable and many were the days when he had little to eat. He collected acorns from the forest, wild fruit and roots which he stewed in a soot-caked cauldron over the fireplace, and from time to time he poached rabbits.

The forest belonged to a baron, as did all the land round about and the village itself. Each year the baron's men collected the rents in form of crops or animals and each able-bodied man was also obliged to give so many days of work a year to keep the baron's particular farmlands in order. No one was allowed to hunt in the forest but the baron. The wild boar, the deer, the foxes and wolves were all his, even the rabbits and stoats and martens.

The villagers were called upon as beaters, when they might be allowed to take home a certain amount of game as a reward when the hunting was good, but this was a special concession. The rabbits that dashed across the fields, the hares that nested in the rye, the rooks and wood pigeons that stole the seed – these were all common prey of the villagers, but all that lived in the forest belonged to the baron.

Josef knew this as well as any man. He knew too that the penalties for being caught poaching were severe. However, such was his nature that he preferred to lie abed half the day instead of tending his cows or his crops and spend half the night slinking among the trees and bracken, setting well-concealed traps which might or might not catch a rabbit. He visited his traps frequently, for fear that one of the keepers might come across a rabbit threshing vainly about, and rarely set them twice in the same place, choosing always the newest rabbit runs and then immediately abandoning them.

It was on a night of the full moon when he caught the black cat in his trap. Astonishment was mingled with instinctive fear at the sight of the savage creature, for it was many years since he had set eyes on such an animal. He had been hardly more than a boy when the last cat was driven from the village and, as he stared into the baleful yellow eyes, narrowed to the moon's brightness, he suddenly recalled those hysterical days, long lost in his memory until now. . .

It had been said then that cats were the agents of the Devil. They converted themselves into witches, they hypnotized people with their stare. At certain times of the year they could fly and their power was both immense and frightening. It was necessary to destroy them.

He remembered being one of a band of youths, armed with sticks and sickles, searching throughout the village while the panic-stricken animals – undoubtedly furnished with second sight – fled before their arrival, betaking themselves to the roofs with supernatural agility, clinging to tree branches, spitting their curses on the heads of those that hunted them. The cats that were caught were taken to the village square, where a huge bonfire had been built, and there they were publicly burned after being exorcized by the priest. A tremendous caterwauling had arisen and many people claimed they could see the evil spirits writhing amid the smoke and ashes as the cats perished.

Josef remembered now those terrible howls and screeches, souls in torment, souls in damnation. He could still almost feel the heat of the blaze on his cheeks, the self-righteous excitement that had gripped him and all who surrounded him, and his heart beat with unusual rapidity as he suddenly recalled those scenes and feelings, the eyes of the captured cat upon him. . .

Moments had passed while these scenes were conjured up in his memory, moments in which he had not removed his gaze from the cat in the trap, and then a terrible fear overtook him, fear of vengeance, fear of bewitchment, so that he rapidly crossed himself and began to evoke the Virgin's protection.

He knew that he should take his club and beat the cat over the head with it. One fierce blow would be enough to kill it. And yet – would it die? Would the evil spirit the hairy frame contained die also with the last convulsive moments, or would it release itself from its agent and seek a new host in himself? He was nearest, he was responsible for the cat's predicament. The witch would surely know this and have its revenge.

Still muttering prayers and agitatedly crossing himself, Josef backed away from the trap, rapidly losing himself amidst the darkness of the ferns and bushes. The cat would surely die within a few days. No one would know anything about it. At least he would not have touched it.

'Mother of God, if you don't allow any evil to befall me I promise never to poach another rabbit from the forest. Mother of God, protect me,' and every prayer he had ever learned fell from his lips as he hurried back to his miserable dwelling, casting aside the two rabbits that were tied to his belt, leaving them to the foxes and the crows.

For days he went nowhere near the forest. He got up early and tended his land, much surprising his neighbours who were used to his lazy ways, and each nightfall he went into the church and spent nearly an hour on his knees, head bowed before the altar. A man whose heart and mind were filled with holy thoughts could never become prey to evil spirits – this was what the priest had promised – and each hour of the day he recited the Lord's Prayer, determined to drive the memory of the cat's angry eyes from his head.

In desperation, because the memory would not leave him, he carved a cross on his door. He was tempted to confess to the priest but was held back by the necessity of giving an explanation of his presence in the forest. He knew he would only rest in peace when he saw the cat dead, for then it could no longer molest him, and he convinced himself that his days and nights of torture were the direct responsibility of the animal in the forest which, until its death, would hold some baleful influence over him.

Therefore, on the sixth day, armed with a stake whose end he had sharpened to a point with the intention of driving it through the animal's heart to be thus certain of its extinction, both physical and spiritual, Josef cautiously returned to the forest.

Against his will, his heart began to beat fast as he recognized the path which had taken him to the trap, and the Lord's Prayer was again on his lips as he forced himself to retread it, filled with dread at the thought of seeing that sorcerer's animal again. He gripped the stake firmly, telling himself it was only a matter of giving one

fierce thrust through the rib cage, for the beast was surely dead, and then . . .

Then he saw Agnes, crouched to the ground, her flaxen hair caressing the creature's body as her fingers worked at the noose embedded in its neck. He saw the claw marks on her arms, the streaks of blood of which she herself was unaware, the animal's lashing tail.

Jaws apart, unable to continue mouthing the magic words that assured his salvation, he silently backed away, clutching the sharp-pointed stake to his breast, no longer remembering it.

Back in the sunlight, away from the mixed shadows of the forest, he stopped to draw breath, and vividly recalled the scene he had just abandoned of the silent child and her angel-fair hair mingled with the cat's raven blackness.

Seven

The cat was too weak to run away, even though it was no longer held captive. It was more dead than alive and whatever instinctive desire for flight it might have felt was extinguished by sheer exhaustion. It just lay there, in the place of its struggles, aware that it was free but no longer caring.

Agnes sat nearby. She was not so much contemplating the cat as participating in its state.

The eyes that never noticed Wilhemina's coaxing gazes and Klaus's scowls were acutely aware of every movement – the almost breathless breaths, the hardly noticeable rise and fall of the hollow flank, the almost unconscious twitch of the tail tip, the slightest retraction of claws – and yet these observed details were understood by her not so much as exterior things, things she could see which expressed the cat's physical condition, but rather as personal experience.

She felt, rather than saw, with her eyes, and with her customary intensity immediately became the thing she observed. Her breath became slight, almost panting; she clenched and unclenched her fingers, while a shudder convulsed her spine every time the cat twitched its tail.

In the gentle sun of that early summer afternoon they both fell asleep, the child stretched out in an attitude similar to that of the cat. They awoke at the same time. The sun had gone and a chill was creeping through the forest, which was darker than before.

Agnes awoke in a daze. She felt very weak and there

was a stiffness in all parts of her body. The cat stared at her. Its eyes were unlike any the child had ever experienced, round and deeply yellow with black centres that grew or shrunk. She immediately felt that her eyes must be the same and touched them with her fingers. There was a pain in the centre of her body, below her ribs, the place where it always hurt when she was hungry. She was suddenly aware of the encroaching darkness and knew it was time to eat. The black creature with the eyes that watched her felt the same pain of hunger.

She stood up. Bits of twig and mould from the forest floor were caught in her hair, while the blood from the scratches had dried on her arms, but she was only aware of the cat whose eyes stared into her own and she picked it up, cradling it in her arms.

The animal let out a fearful hiss and made a slight attempt to escape but then it felt the heat of the child's body, warmer than its own, and its instinctive fear was stilled. It was lulled into a kind of slumber as Agnes made her way back to the village, hurrying as she grew close, knowing she was late. Could Wilhemina have seen her as she crossed the pastures and bypassed the crops she would have been amazed at the expression on her face, the most human smile of contentment which any child or adult could involuntarily produce.

Both Klaus and Wilhemina were sitting at the table, eyeing the bowl in which the cabbage had grown cold, their own dirty plates still before them.

'Do you think something has happened to her?' the woman asked.

'Why should it have?'

'She doesn't usually miss a meal.'

'She'll miss this one if she doesn't come soon. She's not so stupid that she doesn't understand that.'

Klaus had no way of containing his irritability when-

44

ever the child was mentioned, and the food on the table was beginning to annoy him. It annoyed him, too, that his wife still cared enough about the child to worry over her, and greater still was the anger he felt against himself for not having found the courage to turn her out of his home. He was just going to mention again that there would be a place for her at the hall, in the kitchen, when the door was pushed open and Agnes entered.

All three of them immediately understood that something was different. For the first time in years Agnes was actually aware of them, not only aware but cautious, as if she had some secret that she wanted to hide. For the first time she was behaving like a child, in a way that Wilhemina could understand, and although she was bewildered by this change there was also a sudden burst of warmth in her heart which caused her to jump up with a cry.

'Agnes! What have you done? Where have you been? What's happened to you?'

She took hold of the child's hands as she spoke, horror expressed in both voice and eyes at the scratches and blood that criss-crossed her wrists and channelled her forearms. Klaus also sprang up from the table and roughly grasped one of the hands himself.

'Don't be angry with her!' begged his wife, instinctively understanding that for once Agnes was defenceless against them, afraid even.

'Where have you been? How did this happen?' he shouted, his eyes cold with fury.

Would there never be any way of fathoming this inexplicable creature? What kind of trouble would she bring upon them?

'Speak, for God's sake,' he yelled at her. 'You're not deaf. You can hear me. You understand. For once in your life try to tell us.'

'Klaus!' His wife stretched out a restraining hand and hugged the child against her. 'Leave her. You don't know what you're saying. How can she tell us, poor soul? God knows, she must want to say something to us sometimes.'

The man withdrew with an exclamation of mingled disgust and despair.

'Do as you wish. You brought her to the house. Protect her, defend her, waste your warmth on her if you wish, but remember – you're comforting a changeling. She's not your Agnes – our Agnes. Do you even remember her, I wonder? She's a creature Josef brought out of the forest and each day she goes back to the forest and returns to us wilder than before. Look at her!'

He tore her from the woman's arms and thrust her before them both.

'Tonight she comes back like a wild beast that's been in battle. Her dress torn, her arms full of wounds, her hair full of dirt. Suppose she's infected by the madness of the forest animals? Have you thought of that? Is she going to howl and foam at the mouth like a mad dog? Wouldn't it be better to tie her to a stake outside, or lock her up somewhere before she attacks one of us? Only God or the Devil could give an explanation of her actions today.'

'Klaus! Klaus! You don't know what you're saying,' exclaimed Wilhemina, frightened by his raging words, stabbed by his reference to their daughter but incapable of resisting the child's sudden need of her.

The man flung himself out of the cottage and while he was gone Wilhemina gently drew Agnes to the fireplace and gave her a jug of milk, noticing with what hunger she gulped it down. She filled a bowl with water from the big iron pot that stood simmering over the ashes and found some rags for cleaning the wounds.

At first Agnes resisted her attentions, dragging her

hands away, but then it seemed that the warm water soothed her for she allowed Wilhemina to do as she would without further struggle, and the woman wonderingly tried to understand why sometimes this strange child could feel pain and other times she could not. She combed the dirt and twigs out of her hair while Agnes swallowed the stewed cabbage that was her supper, leaning against her legs, the hair spread across her lap, and Wilhemina forgot her fear and her husband's rage, wistfully imagining how sweetly peaceful life would be if Agnes were always so yielding and biddable.

She left her half asleep, as she thought, by the fireplace while she gathered up the things from the table and saw to a few simple duties, but when she next glanced towards Agnes, a soft smile already on her lips, assured that she would find her quite asleep, she was gone!

She drew in her breath sharply, for she had seen and heard nothing and hardly a moment had passed, and immediately all Klaus's prophecies and threats hammered in her thoughts. She clutched at her heart, feeling its suddenly rapid beats.

'Agnes! Agnes!' she called, running out into the now full darkness of the night.

The moon was in its first quarter, the sky was cloudy, and she could make out very little beyond the bulky shadows of the neighbouring cottages and a vague glimmer on the cabbages in the garden. For a second she thought she saw something move, for a second she thought she heard hurried footsteps and some kind of animal sound, but then there was only darkness and silence and she was afraid to walk out any farther, fear of the inexplicable and her own hammering heart paralysing her.

Eight

Agnes had rushed off to where she had hidden the cat among the rushes beside the pond. She had the milk jug in one hand, in which she had deliberately left a small quantity for the cat, and a chunk of rye bread in the other. When she heard the woman calling her, she crouched down and was very still and soon she knew that she had gone back indoors.

The cat had not moved from where she had laid it. Hunger, thirst and pain had completely destroyed its energies. A certain warmth had seeped through to it while Agnes carried it in her arms but the moment she left it among the rushes it immediately abandoned itself once again to its weakness.

Agnes took the cat from the hiding place and laid it on the grass. She began dipping her fingers in the jug and letting the few drops of milk thus obtained drip onto the cat's jaws. She did this for some time with no obvious result. The cat just lay there, its yellow eyes half closed, as if unaware of her actions or even her presence. Agnes licked her lips, unconsciously willing the animal to do the same, and then she pulled it on to her lap, nursing it in her left arm, bending so closely over it that it could feel her breath in its nostrils.

When it began to feel warm again it grew aware of the milk, damp on its jaws and nose. Painfully the swollen tongue rasped out to clean itself. Agnes then poured a small amount into her cupped hand at which the animal began to lick. It could not drink rapidly because of its

49

injured throat but the slow movements were a source of satisfaction to her. Time after time she repeated the action until the milk was all gone and then she brought water from the pond in her cupped hands at which the cat lapped too, licking and licking her palms and fingers.

At last it was satisfied. It stood up shakily and tried to stretch itself. In the half-light Agnes could hardly make anything of its bedraggled appearance. In a moment it was questing tentatively towards her, seeking the warmth her body offered.

She put her hand under its stomach, feeling the brittle hair against her fingers, and lifted it onto her lap. It immediately curled up and dug its head into her body, prodding here and there with its muzzle, and then its front paws began to knead against her, too, as a primitive song of contentment rose in its throat. For the first time Agnes heard the song of the cat, deep, gentle, rhythmic, keeping pace with the movement of its claws.

The sound entered deep into her body, though consciously she neither felt nor heard it. It was within her, part of her, entrancing, lulling, pacifying the deepest, loneliest part of her. She shut her eyes, completely surrendering herself to the cat's contentment, her arms locked round it, her head and shoulders imperceptibly rocking from side to side.

Klaus, returning from the ale-house where he had gone to rid himself of his anger with a few tankards of beer, saw the slight figure beside the pond. The moon was no longer entangled by the clouds and it shed a dim but steadfast light across his garden, glimmering on the smooth pond water, slightly touching the child's fair hair.

He stopped in his tracks. He had drunk his anger away and was feeling torpid. For a while he had forgotten about the child but this unexpected sight of her renewed the dull sense of irritation that irked him whenever she was near.

'What can she be doing now?' he mumbled to himself.

He did not really want to know, he did not really care and, besides, the strangest thing she might do was no longer strange to him. He remembered how she stroked stones for hours, completely still but for the movement of her fingers; he remembered how at one time his wife feared she might fall into the pond and drown and how, more than once, he had hoped that she would. The water tempted her uncannily.

He intended to continue his way but his very irritation prodded him to go and see what she was up to. She would not even see him, anyway. She never did.

As he got close he saw that her eyes were shut and that something was held in her arms, something very dark leaning close against her, but he could not make out what it was. Even as he puzzled, slowly because the ale had made his mind as heavy as his body, he became aware of the muted sound that rose from her presence, whether from between her own closed lips or from the black thing that shadowed half her body he could not tell. But he stopped and went no nearer, not wanting to know, afraid to know.

He almost ran back to the cottage where his wife anxiously greeted him. 'Have you seen Agnes? Is she out there? I looked earlier but I couldn't find her.'

'No. I haven't seen her.'

He slammed the door as he spoke and pulled across the wedge that bolted it. Then he turned fiercely on his wife.

'If she's out there she can stay out there. Why didn't you go to find her yourself?'

'I was afraid.'

She shrugged her shoulders helplessly, unable to explain the feeling that had overcome her.

51

'I was afraid,' she repeated, unable to to meet her husband's gaze, and they both went to bed without speaking another word.

At some hour in the night Wilhemina was awakened. She knew that a sound had disturbed her although, when she listened, only silence answered her. Had Agnes been trying to open the door, she wondered? She dared not disturb her husband and therefore did not move, but although her ears were strained for the sound again she fell asleep without hearing it.

Nine

In the first few days the cat needed all Agnes's attention in order to survive. It was so weak that it could hardly walk but just because Agnes did nothing but hold it in her arms and nurse it, the close association with a human being, which in normal circumstances would have been impossible, rid the cat of all its fear and wildness.

It was a young animal, hardly more than a kitten, descendant of the few survivors that had escaped the village so many years earlier. When Agnes found it, it was as wild as any creature in the forest, as cautious as the fox, as silent as the lynx, as savage as the boar, but unlike any of these animals an inherent claim to domesticity lay dormant in its blood. It would never have sought the company of mankind but having unexpectedly been drawn into it, and in such a defenceless condition, its reaction was less negative than would have been the fox's, the lynx's or the boar's.

At first it could swallow nothing but milk and water but after a while it was able to eat the bread Agnes mixed with the milk. Frequent feeding brought the shine and silkiness back to its blue-black coat. Only the sore ring round its neck spoilt its appearance and caused annoyance. The hair where the noose had dug so deeply into its skin was completely rubbed away. The noose had worked right into the flesh itself and these wounds, together with the deep tears caused by the frantic clawings of the desperate animal, took a long time to heal. In some parts the hair began to grow again but the scar left by the noose

53

never faded. It formed a complete circle round the jawbones and behind the ears.

The cat was as black as the crows that came to steal from the farmers' fields. Its coat was as soft as the grass and as smooth as rose petals. Agnes liked nothing better than to run her fingers from the top of its head to the tip of its tail and the cat responded to her constant caresses by pushing its head under her hand for further attention, stretching and squirming with delight.

Agnes kept the cat a secret, for the first time aware that both she and it existed in a world inhabited by other beings who she instinctively felt could in some way intrude upon their relationship and destroy it. While too weak to move, she kept it in the rushes beyond the pond at night and as soon as the sun was up she was away to the forest, the cat tight in her arms, a jug filled with milk she had stolen from the cow before Klaus had even opened his eyes.

One morning when she came to look for the cat, the sun still a red glow behind the early mist and only the rushes standing straight and green beneath it, it was gone. The place where it had lain was crushed but cold. Agnes knelt there, feeling the cold hollow with her fingers as if it could give her knowledge of its absent occupant.

They were terrible moments, in which the emotions of three days verged on utter destruction, but suddenly the cat's head appeared between the rushes beyond the nest. Its big yellow eyes stared up at her.

Miaow!

The abyss vanished at the sound and if Agnes had been capable of laughing she would have laughed out loud.

It was then that she became afraid, afraid that this other self would vanish like the mist that was already disintegrating all about her. She gave the cat its milk, cupped in her hand as usual, and carried it away to a place in the forest where the hours passed uncounted. At nightfall she came back alone.

In the forest she found a tree with a hollow in its trunk, among the roots. Perhaps it had been a badger's den. It was warm and dry and smelt of all the safe things Agnes knew. She put the cat in this hollow and dragged some broken branches across the opening of sufficient weight and thickness to ensure that the cat could neither slip through them nor push them aside. The cat had no objection to this den and, later, it was no longer necessary for her to block its entrance.

With the first light of the sun filtering through the leafy shadows, Agnes was there to meet the cat which came running towards her, mewing a greeting, flicking its stiffly held tail and rubbing its head against her. Agnes would pick it up and rub her own nose and head against its chest, gently pummelling its soft underparts as she held it on its back in the crook of her arm.

Then came the ritual of the food. It was never sufficient for Agnes to put down a bowl with the milk and bread and let the cat eat its fill. It was necessary to crumble the bread in the palm of her hand, pour a little of the milk over it and thus offer it to the cat, her main pleasure lying in the feel of the cat's tongue rasping her skin as it ate.

Her relationship with the cat was extremely intense. She lived only for the sensations its nearness or touch produced in her and she could not differentiate between the cat's feelings and her own. She was the cat. The cat was her. It was only as her love grew stronger and, with love, a growing awareness of her own existence that she occasionally realized that the cat had a personality of its own.

When she glimpsed this truth – very rarely and usually in too intangible a way for her to grasp at, except as in a

55

stab of momentary confusion – she would need to hold it very close. When it was purring on her lap, nearly asleep, Agnes entered a state of blissful trance, such as a baby might feel, gently rocking in its mother's arms.

The cat was strong and playful. When it was freed from the child's embrace it would pounce after butterflies and shadows, pawing the air with outstretched claws. It would dash in circles, chasing its tail, flash up and down a tree-trunk in a trice, leap from a bough to the ground and battle with ferns and dandelions. Once it pounced on an unsuspecting bird. With the little creature fluttering vainly between its jaws, the cat turned to face Agnes with lashing tail, its whole expression changed. When she made a move towards it, it slunk away, hurrying to its den at the foot of the tree, and when this happened it was like a great door slamming down, leaving her in darkness.

Usually, the cat's movements delighted her. She never tired of watching the supple muscles ripple beneath the shiny black skin; the flicking, waving tail which moved in accordance with the cat's mood and expressed its every change of feeling; the back and forward inflection of the ears; the skilled co-ordination of every nerve and tendon throughout the slim, dark frame.

Soon she felt herself capable of the self-same movements. A lightness would come to her heart with the urge to express the same sense of freedom demonstrated by the cat. Instinctively she began to dance, at once mastering the natural rhythms her body possessed. Her tireless observation of the cat's movements subconsciously served her now and her bare feet hardly seemed to touch the earth as she floated gently or whirled wildly about an open space in the forest.

Sometimes she would dance until she fell to the ground, collapsing in an unmoving heap, having unwittingly worked herself into an exhausted trance. The cat would pause in its games and come to sniff at her and, if she stayed unmoving for very long, it would often curl up beside her, some part of its body resting against her own, and sing itself into slumber.

Ten

As the weeks went by the cat wrought a subtle change in
Agnes. Wilhemina felt it but it was not sufficiently
obvious for her to be able to explain it even to herself, let
alone to Klaus who answered with a curse every time the
child's name was mentioned. Was it in the expression of
her eyes, was it just in the aura about her that seemed
less forbidding, was it that sometimes she seemed almost
to be smiling? She asked and asked herself as she sat with
her tasks, often alone, wondering where Agnes was, what
she was doing, what had happened to make her different.

Agnes herself was aware of no change. She was so
rarely aware of herself anyway that it was as if for
herself she did not exist. She could not judge any change
of feeling or behaviour because she never analysed herself.
She had only two states of being, one of desolation and
one of non-existence. This latter was her most common
state, when she became a frog or a tree or the wind in the
cornfields. It was her escape from the eternal unhappiness
that dominated her conscious mind and when the priest
had exclaimed that she was soulless, in his way he was
right.

She had instinctively fought against the 'Agnes' in her
and as each year passed her evasion of reality was ever
more successful. She would not be Agnes. She would be
nothing, or everything, for by merging into the everything
all about her she successfully lost all sense of personal
identity. There was no way of halting her, no way of even
understanding her and trying to find a way.

But then the small miracle happened. She found the cat in the forest, recognized in its distress a desolation equal to her own, and instinctively clung to it, like attracted to like.

When she brought it home and felt its brittle body warm against her own, for the first time she was aware of sensations in herself which had nothing to do with loneliness. For the first time there was the feeling that she was sharing something, giving some part of herself, the essential warmth of her body which mingled with that of the cat. She was not being the cat then, although at first sight she had felt its pain. She was giving it the protection it needed, the protection she herself constantly sought and had only ever found in self-annihilation.

When she hid the cat among the rushes it was not because she thought that Klaus or Wilhemina might not let her keep it. The man and woman did not exist for her to that extent and no thought of them entered her mind at all. Her action was an instinctive desire to keep the creature for herself, to share it with no one, and while Wilhemina bathed her arms and offered her food, the only awareness she had had was of the warmth and comfort she could give to that other creature as soon as she was free.

Feeding the cat with the milk was a repetition of the previous action of feeding herself, one of the few conscious acts that was pleasurable to her. She knew that if she did not eat she felt a pain in her body. She did not know that if she did not eat she would die. Therefore, it was not in an effort to save the cat's life that she had first fed it. It was because she had wanted to give it the pleasure that she herself experienced at the sight and smell of food.

It was afterwards, when the cat had drunk and stretched itself and she had taken it onto her lap in order to give it more warmth, that the strangest, newest feeling of all came over her. This was when the cat began to purr. The vibrations of its song of contentment penetrated.to the depth of her being, stirring her in a way that nothing had stirred her since she had come from the forest herself, taking her back to a time before memory existed and instinct alone remembered.

The cat's song was like a lullaby and she knew, without knowing, that somewhere, in some distant, intangible time, such a song had existed before.

In those moments, while the cat's paws kneaded and its throat swelled with lullaby, Agnes regained her soul, for the first time feeling herself capable of loving and needing to be loved.

And this was the change that Wilhemina could sense in the child and yet not understand. Had she followed Agnes to the forest, had she been able to see her with the cat, then she would have understood and her heart would have been gladdened. But only Josef ever followed Agnes, without her knowledge, and what he saw in his ignorance was witchcraft.

Eleven

That summer a crowd of strangers unexpectedly trudged into the village. They were a group of men, women and children, fifteen souls in all, carrying bundles and cooking utensils, weariness and despair grimed with the dust into their faces. Women and children ran to meet them, dogs barked and wagged their tails even while they growled at the strangers, who were conducted bodily towards the main square where at last they were allowed to sit on the ground among their few possessions. The headman of the village was sent for and by the time he had been brought back from one of his fields most of the villagers had learned of the strangers' arrival and had left their tools and tasks to find out why they had come.

The greeting they were given was not very heart-warming for the villagers prided themselves on their secluded position, where until now neither the plague nor the soldiers had found them. They knew from the rare traveller's visit that everywhere in the land villages were being pillaged and burned by the reckless hordes of mercenaries fighting in the name of the emperor.

For more than ten years now the countryside had been suffering their rapacious booty-hunting and heartless cruelty. Who or where the enemy was they had only the vaguest idea. People were dying and being left homeless in the name of Christ and the Emperor; this was all they understood, and once when a stranger had wandered by chance into their valley, with the look of a soldier about him, they had butchered him without a second thought,

fearfully certain that he had been foraging for the army
and would bring the whole horde down upon them if they
allowed him to return.

The fifteen souls now gathered in the square in front of
the church instinctively understood the mood of the
crowd growing about them. The men had come with
scythes and pitchforks; there was the glint of axe or
knife in the women's hands and even the children were
searching about for stones which they tossed impatiently
in their hands.

The spokesman of the group, a broad, grey-haired man called Martin, with bruises and grazes on his face and a rough bandage round his head, had gone into the house with the priest and the headman and while they talked no one was disposed to violence, waiting the result of their parleying. But the antagonistic undercurrent was felt by all and a fearful silence fell upon everyone, waiting in the sunlight before the church. A small child belonging to the strangers began to whimper and its mother pulled it into her arms to hush its noise. This small action gave rise to momentary murmuring, then silence fell again.

At last the three men came out again, the stranger the tallest among them, and all faces turned anxiously towards them. The priest spoke.

'These people say they have been on the road for five days. Their village was burned to the ground by robbers, their cattle driven off, most of their neighbours brutally murdered. They say they have seen no further sign of the bandits but are afraid to return to what is left of their homes for fear of finding them still occupied by the invaders. They ask permission to rest here for a few days. Some of them have wounds which need tending. Two of the children are sick. They are prepared to work in exchange for anything we can offer them. More than anything they need food.'

Hardly had he finished speaking when everyone began to talk at once, questions, complaints and doubts issuing from every throat. So many hungry people would need a lot of feeding. What kind of illness had sickened the children? How could they be sure that the bandits were not behind them, that it was not even a diabolical plan of the self-same rogues?

'If the bandits attack us then we shall have seven extra men to help defend our homes,' the priest answered them. 'And at least we have been forewarned of their possible advent.'

'We'll set up some outposts,' said the headman, 'by the road and the river. If anyone comes to attack us we shall know about it in good time.'

Several plans were discussed and agreed upon and in the meantime the weary refugees were shown into the public meeting house and told they could lodge there for the next few days. This was a big hall with a thatched roof where the women and girls forgathered with their distaffs and spindles to gossip and sing while they worked in the evenings, when the young men would wander in to watch them and sometimes join in the conversation. They would pretend to help the young women with the flax and cheeks would grow rosier and eyes brigher as the evening passed in laughter and joking and sometimes in song. Once Wilhemina had always been among the women with her spinning but since Agnes had thrown such a shadow over her days she preferred to stay at home.

Klaus only went to the ale-house, which was a rowdier meeting place than the other and which, that night, was packed with people seeking information from the new arrivals. Klaus was there, having left Wilhemina at the meeting house with their contribution to the strangers' welfare; a pile of straw for bedding, some bread and a basketful of plums from the trees in their gardens.

Josef was sitting at one of the tavern tables, mulling over a tankard of beer which had been paid for by one of the strangers. He had lost count of what he had drunk that night and was only half awake to the conversation being shouted on every side. It was a big night for the villagers, dulled by the never-ending monotony of their day-to-day existence; a night of tension, too, for beneath their surface jollity was the doubt and fear that caught at them whenever they were abrubtly reminded of the disasters that might any day overtake them, just as the strangers had been overcome.

There was talk of war, of violence, burning and death. Young men bragged of how they would defend their homes, their faces red with excitement. Some of the older ones told them to content themselves with tilling the soil and not to seek the doubtful excitements of war.

Martin, who seemed the most respected among the strangers, began to talk of all the disasters that had befallen their village in the last ten years or so until its final destruction, marvelling that this little place in the valley should be such a haven of peace when they had been struggling on the borders of hell itself for so long.

Bandits, plague, soldiers. Each disaster had taken its toll of them in turn and in the wake of each had come hunger and death.

'Whenever we began to think that at last we had left the worst times behind, whenever it seemed as though the cows would start to give milk again, the trees would begin to produce fruit, whenever we'd broken our backs getting the soil to give us at least one good harvest, some new disaster always befell us. For two winters running we had soldiers quartering with us.' He grunted ironically. 'They were supposed to be defending us and by the time they'd done that they'd murdered half the able-bodied men and reduced us all to penury. You don't know how lucky you are here, living with such peace.'

'We're all God-fearing men in this village,' mumbled Josef who was nearest to him. 'There's no truck with the new religion here.'

'New religion, old religion! It's all the same to those devils once they pour down on you. They bang you over the head with their cudgels before asking you what you believe. They only worship the demon themselves.'

While speaking, this stranger had attracted the attention of nearly everybody there. His weary, pain-marked features could not disguise the open, intelligent expression which set him apart from most of the people round him, making him a natural spokesman, a leader in any circumstances. Klaus had been drawn to him without knowing why, instinctively understanding that he was the kind of man some would respect and some would envy, comparing him with his fellow villager who, having said very little, had yet managed to impress him as a rogue.

Martin had nothing more to say. He sat down, holding his head in his hands as if it ached, and soon afterwards Klaus went home, tired of so much talk of disaster. A number of others followed his example and soon only a few remained at the tavern, Josef among them, drinking down their last tankards of the night. Josef was loth to move. He had drunk far too much and was only jogged into wakefulness by a man on the bench beside him who was sharply insisting, 'It all started with that woman, I tell you. But you've never been willing to admit it.'

At first Josef thought the man was addressing him and muzzily answered, 'What woman? I don't know anything about a woman,' realizing his mistake when another voice, Martin's, answered truculently, 'Can you never let sleeping dogs lie?'

'We never had any trouble before then,' insisted the first. 'We were as peaceful and happy as these people here. God-fearing, except for one or two of us.'

'Forget it.'

'Forget it! Forget it, when we're still being punished, still under her curse. Do you really believe that this last trouble was just a coincidence? Until we find her body and put a stake through her heart, we'll never know peace again. It's what we should have done when she disappeared. We should have looked for the body. You insisted then that it didn't matter, and now you can see how wrong you were, but you won't admit it.'

Josef pricked his ears. 'What woman are you talking about?' he interrupted.

'It's an old story,' Martin answered, brushing off the question.

'Old, perhaps, but unfinished,' insisted the other, as if determined to draw him out. 'Still, you were among those who defended her.'

'Defend her! I didn't defend her. All I said at the

time was that we shouldn't be hasty and, in spite of all that's happened, I still say she wasn't a witch.'

Bitterness and disgust were expressed in his weary features. He obviously disliked the man who seemed determined to harry him.

'Then how do you explain her disappearance, the plague that came afterwards and all the rest? We've had nothing but misfortune ever since her body disappeared off the scaffold.'

'Perhaps, instead of a witch's curse, it's God's punishment.'

'What's this? What's this?' cried Josef. In spite of his half-stupor, his eyes were suddenly hard with interest and he was unaware of the contempt with which Martin regarded both his companions.

'It'll be eight years this autumn that it happened,' answered the other. 'I remember it well because my eldest boy died from the pains in the stomach she induced in him because he was among those who discovered her tricks and gave evidence against her. He would have been eighteen now. Tell him, Martin. You saw him. You were there and you're better with words than I am.'

But Martin was silent and Josef looked anxiously from face to face, impatient to hear more. Martin gazed at him scornfully, then said, 'What do you want to hear? How we tortured her to make her confess, or what led us to believe she was a witch?'

'Everything,' he answered eagerly, indifferent to the man's expression.

'Then you'd better ask Sebastian here. He brought the subject up, perhaps because he was both accuser and executioner. I have been trying to forget it ever since.' And he got up, pushing his tankard aside, and went away.

Josef sidled closer to the man still sitting on the bench. 'Well, then,' he said softly. 'You tell me.'

Twelve

Sebastian told the story as he knew it, embellishing or disguising the facts as it suited him, with none of the other man's conscience to worry him. Josef heard only Sebastian's version of the time when a village went berserk and it was as prejudiced an account as any that might have been given of that day's events. The truth had died with the woman who had been branded as a witch. . . .

*

No one had ever liked her. To start with she was different from everyone else, with jet black hair and eyes equally dark, eyes that gleamed defiance and coldness at nearly everyone who dared to meet her gaze. Nothing much was known of her beyond the fact that her parents and brother had died within a few days of each other of some mysterious complaint when she was thirteen or fourteen. Since then she had shunned everyone, caring for herself in the hovel on the outskirts of the village and mocking even the priest's attempts to keep her in the fold.

Her only friend was the village midwife and cure-all, an old woman called Hella, with whom she would go to the fields and woods to find the plants and roots she used for her medicines. Occasionally she would help her cure a sick child or poultice a broken limb and when Hella died she was the only one who understood her cures and crafts.

Few people would go to her for assistance and those who did went in secret or shamefully. The boys spied on her and played tricks on her, mixing up her herbs, breaking her cooking utensils, spitefully mischievous in every way. They said later that she danced in the moonlight, completely alone, and talked in a loud voice to an invisible companion.

No one knew where the baby came from, whether it was hers, some other woman's, or a child of the Devil. It was rumoured that shortly before the infant was first seen and heard that a person, or persons, had been in her hovel one night, but no one could describe them or even say if they were male or female. The child in no way looked like its presumed mother, being as fair as a summer's day. Every kind of rumour hummed through the village but the woman remained aloof from the voices, as always.

When the baby was some six months old a sickness struck most of the nursing children. They grew weaker and weaker, then died, but *her* baby was seen to be as plump and as pretty as ever. The women began to whisper among themselves and discovered that those of the stricken families had at some time or another been cursed by her.

From then on they were afraid of her. If she crossed their path they hurriedly looked away, refusing to meet her gaze, frightened of those powerful black eyes. Men were rough with her and deliberately insulting and yet, although she was surrounded by enemies who would not lift a hand to help her, neither she nor the child ever lacked food or clothing.

When the pigs and the cows fell sick, dying at an alarming rate, people began to look for a culprit. Then it was that the boys produced their evidence, as varied as it was frightening; the moonlight dances, the one-sided conversations . . . they had even seen her throw herself down and foam at the mouth! The women talked of her curses, of the fearful sensation that overtook them whenever she was close, and some young men spoke of having

70

seen her with a mysteriously disguised figure on several occasions in the fields, a figure impossible to identify as either man or woman. The priest already knew she was condemned to eternal hellfire because she had deliberately turned away from the church and he had not a good word to say for her.

Sebastian's son fell sick only a few hours after he had given his evidence against her. Such was his agony that the desperate father went to the witch's house and begged for her assistance. But she refused to look at him, accusing him of being her greatest tormentor, saying that he had probably eaten too much raw fruit from the orchards. He offered to make amends, to give her anything she asked for, but she pushed him out of her hovel, telling him to pray instead.

Within a short time everyone knew how the witch was tormenting the child. They crowded into Sebastian's home to see with their own eyes how he writhed and howled. There was obviously no pretence in his sickness. Even the priest was impressed and when Sebastian cried that until her evil presence was destroyed there could be no hope for his son's salvation – and perhaps that of the other boys who had spoken against her – everyone was loud in agreement.

The few cautious voices were overridden and when these few saw how the tide had definitely turned against her and that if they persisted in their weak defence they were likely to be accused as accomplices, they remained silent. A fever had taken hold of the villagers, distressed by so many hardships and now frightened at the sight of this child dying in agony. They rushed in a body upon their chosen culprit, led by Sebastian, while the priest stayed behind, trying to palliate the effects of witchcraft with prayer.

She was too proud to beg for mercy. Perhaps she

knew they had no mercy in their hearts to which she could appeal. The children's lies and exaggerations were obviously believed, the women had every reason to be resentful at the sight of her chubby-cheeked child. It seemed that each person had a reason for hating her.

Like a wild boar when cornered by a pack of lusting dogs snapping at heels and flanks and head, that flings itself back into the fray though it knows it must go under, she defied her accusers, daring them to harm her, heaping every kind of curse upon their heads, laughing wildly at their obvious fear to disguise the terror that gripped her, and calling upon the Devil to hear her and be revenged.

She would confess to nothing although they tortured her, her curses growing wilder and more fearful with each new pain, and all the time the small child that belonged to her crouched in a corner of the hovel, forgotten by everyone, its pleasant little world falling asunder at the sight and sound of so much pain and brutality.

Sebastian was impatient. His boy was burning with fever and convulsed with pain. He knew the witch could save him if she wanted to. He believed in her powers more than he believed in the power of God.

'Only save him,' he begged, 'and we'll be merciful. There's still time to save both him and yourself.'

'He's being punished for his lies,' she gasped into his flushed face. 'He deserves whatever happens to him.'

She was dragged out of the hovel, which was immediately set on fire. For a while the child stayed petrified in its corner, watching the flames flicker and grow and leap from walls to roof, until a sense of self-preservation sent it scuttling outside before it was overcome. The people were pushing, jostling and dragging their victim down the road which led out of the village. By the time

the child had finished rubbing its smoke-swollen eyes
they were almost out of sight. But it began to toddle in
their wake, for that way had its mother been taken, dried
tears on its face which was dark red from the heat of the
flames.

There was a tree at the crossroads about half a mile
from the village from which, legend had it, a witch had
previously been hanged. There was no stopping the
people now. Fear and fury had reached its pitch. The
rope was already about the woman's neck and two
young men were in the tree with Sebastian, only too
anxious to act as hangmen.

By the time the small child reached the place, the
villagers were already hurrying back to their homes, as
if suddenly ashamed or fearful for themselves. They did
not even notice the child whose outstretched hands could
just reach the soles of its mother's naked feet.

*

When the villagers returned later that day and found
the body gone they took this as the final proof of witchcraft. There were a number of uneasy minds, for it would
have been more comforting to discover an ordinary
human body dangling there, quite dead, but so convinced
were they that the Devil had been at work among them
that it did not occur to anyone to search for their victim
in the nearby forest or even to imagine she was still alive.
The child had disappeared too. It had probably been an
incubus.

The boy died the same day, at about the same hour
that they were hanging the witch.

Thirteen

Josef did not sleep that night but lay tossing and turning on the dirty straw, Sebastian's story going round and round in his head. Nothing could keep him from connecting the witch's offspring with the silent child that had come from the forest. He fought in vain against believing it. He did not want to believe that he had been watching the daughter of a witch all these days and that, through the cat, he was unwittingly connected with her. But however hard he tried to dismiss the connection, his heart throbbed ever more wildly until he groaned in despair and knew that he could evade the truth no longer.

Agnes was the offspring of that terrible woman Sebastian had talked about and, sooner or later, the same things would come to pass in this village as had passed in the other.

What must he do? Dared he denounce her? Would she ever discover how often he had spied on her and put a curse on him?

If he were to go to the priest with his story a lot of awkward questions might be asked. What was he doing in the forest? How did the child come to possess the cat? Why had he not reported these things sooner? His poaching activities might come to light and this was almost as serious as being accused of witchcraft. And so he groaned and tossed and wished he had never set the trap in the forest which had caught the cat.

Just before it was light Josef rose and went outside. There was the usual early summer mist lying over the village and across the fields so that most things could be seen hazily, and the fruit trees in the neighbouring gardens looked trunkless. Josef's head ached with tiredness and the effects of the ale and at that early moment, when even the cocks had hardly decided to untuck their crests, it seemed as though the whole world lay under the spell of witchcraft. He could not even hear the rustle of the animals in their stables or the song of the first awakened bird. Had everything stopped living overnight so that the devils and spirits that inhabited the darkness could play their games undisturbed and unobserved, and had he, never usually awake at this hour just on the verge of dawn, accidentally discovered their secret?

At that moment he could believe anything and his whole body shook with fear and the chill of the early morning. Even as he listened, he began to hear the first daylight sounds. The call of a bird, the chip-chip of a thrush breaking a snail's shell open against a stone, the gentle low of a waking cow and, at last, the brazen call of his neighbour's cockerel. Then voice answered voice, sound echoed sound. The sun was up. The mist was beginning to disperse, leaving only the dew on the grass, but a coldness had entered Josef's heart, born of dread.

*

He found Sebastian later that morning, drew him aside and told him what he suspected, keeping to himself his own knowledge of the cat and giving only the child's history since her mysterious appearance among them and his discovery of her playing in the forest with the cat.

'But why do you tell this to me?' Sebastian demanded. 'How many other people have you told?'

'No one. No one. Not even the priest knows what I've seen.'

'Why not? If you really believe she's a witch surely the thing to do is to inform the priest.'

'It wasn't until I heard your own story last night that the truth finally came to me. She must be that woman's daughter.'

'Rubbish!'

'Then how do you explain the disappearance of a child from one village and the appearance of a child in another about the same age and at the same time?'

'No one ever knew if she really was her daughter,' Sebastian reminded him. 'She was just there one day. We all saw her though we hadn't seen her before.'

'Just there! And she was just here one day, too.'

Sebastian was silent after that. Josef could not guess at his thoughts but he was obviously greatly occupied by them and seemed to have forgotten the existence of his companion. Some time went by before he finally said, 'Tell me about the man Klaus. What kind of person is he?'

Josef shrugged, puzzled by the question.

'He's strong, honest, a good man in his way. With the luck of the Devil, I'd say!'

'Why would you say that?'

'Bah! His animals are always the best. Others grow sick or break their legs, but his always throw good calves and give plenty of milk. They last through the winter like no one else's. And as for his fruit trees! I've never seen such apples and quinces. The only luck he never had was with his offspring. Only one daughter and she died, as I've told you.'

'Why don't you take me to see this Agnes? Let me judge for myself whether or not she's a witch.'

Josef hesitated. In fact he was frightened, more than he had ever been before. If previously he had only half-believed his suspicions, now he was certain, and the less he had to do with the witch the better it would be.

'I don't know. I don't know,' he muttered, shaking his head. 'Wouldn't it be better if we told the priest and left things in his hands?'

'If that's how you feel, why come to me with your tale? I'm a stranger here, after all. Why should I be interested?'

'I thought you might come with me to the priest to verify my suspicions and tell your story again. One of us he might not believe but, with two of us, he would have to take notice.'

'And what satisfaction will you get out of that?' sneered Sebastian. 'Go on with you then. Tell the priest. Repeat my story if you like, if it will ease your conscience. But he might ask you why you haven't gone to him sooner.'

'Then what should I do? What would be best?'

Sebastian put an arm round his shoulder, as if to comfort him. 'If you're interested, I've got a plan. But first I want to see this Agnes. Until I see her there's nothing to be done.'

Josef was only too anxious now to let someone share the burden which had been weighing him down for weeks. He led Sebastian to the forest, his heart beginning to pound with dread as they grew close to the place where Agnes was usually to be found.

His imagination could go no further than the horrific descriptions of hell which the priest frequently thundered at the erring villagers – souls writhing in eternal agony while the Devil gloatingly contemplated the cauldrons of bubbling oil and fire from which there was no salvation. Witches and demons of every kind had haunted him since he had first seen Agnes with the cat and he was longing to throw off his connection with them both, powerless to do so because he believed himself to be part of the things that happened in the forest.

His incessant need to spy on Agnes, his inability to think of anything but her, the utter certainty that he was within her power, had completely weakened him but now, for the first time since his lonely, self-imposed vigil had begun, a sense of release was beginning to lighten his heart and muddled conscience. Sebastian was younger and less afraid. His soul was innocent of any connection, except remotely, with the two beings in the forest and he would know how to save him from them. So although his heart pounded with its usual dread, there was also a certain hope that somehow, soon, his nightmare visions would be ended.

*

She was there as usual, sitting cross-legged in a sunny patch beneath the trees, hugging herself, swaying slowly from side to side. The cat sat only a few lengths away, surveying her, its sharp ears pricked, its eyes narrowed. The scar from the noose was plainly visible due to the way the sun's rays struck down on the black fur.

Suddenly the cat was aware of the watchers. It caught either sound or smell of them and, with one rapid movement, was away, covering the open glade with a few effortless bounds and disappearing among the bushes on the other side.

It was not the cat's behaviour which astonished them but Agnes's, whose actions were a repetition of the animal's. It was as if two cats had fled simultaneously, instead of a cat and a child, and afterwards neither Josef nor Sebastian could have sworn whether they had seen Agnes running upright or on all fours, so close in symmetry were all her movements with those of the cat.

In seconds, both of them had vanished.

Fourteen

Sebastian's motives were purely mercenary. He had at once seen, as Josef would never have done, how he could take advantage of an unusual opportunity. He had come desperate and penniless into this village, quite by chance, to be suddenly presented with a ghost from the past. In no time at all he had dragged the whole story from the old man because, for a while, on seeing the mark of the noose round the cat's throat a chill had seized his heart. Could this beautiful black animal be a reincarnation of the woman who was hanged from the tree, its throat still scarred by the rope that had strangled the life from her?

Afterwards, when Josef had told him the truth, he inwardly laughed at his own gullibility but it was this strange coincidence that gave him the most important piece of evidence to support the claim he intended to broadcast throughout the village should Klaus not be reasonable about paying for his silence.

He said nothing to Josef about his intentions, not knowing him well enough to trust him and sensing him to be something of a rogue, but he told him to take him to Klaus, after impressing on him the need to keep silence until it was necessary to speak out.

'You must never let anyone know the cat was caught in one of your snares,' he insisted. 'You must see for yourself that it was all part of the Devil's plan. The witch died on the scaffold, with the marks of the rope burned into her throat, and when the daughter resuscitated her in animal form it was only natural that she should come back to life as she had died, choking in a noose.'

As it was very convenient for Josef to believe this, for it immediately released him from all responsibility in the affair and at long last relieved his tortured conscience, he was only too willing to keep silent. He came back from the forest with a different gait. All his tiredness had fallen away. All his fear was gone. This stranger, Sebastian, had saved him from the fires of hell and he was anxious to help him as far as it lay within his power.

Klaus received them both with dour suspicion. He had never liked Josef, knowing him for an idler and wastrel, and he instinctively felt that his new companion had even worse defects. He did not like the way Sebastian seemed to be summing up the value of his goods, eyeing his cattle and poultry with hardly disguised satisfaction, and sharply demanded, 'Well, what do you want?' with none of the usual courtesies.

'It's a long story,' answered Sebastian smoothly, unperturbed by Klaus's rough tone, convinced that it would only too soon be changed. 'Be patient while I tell it from the beginning.'

Wilhemina came close before the tale was much begun. They were near the pond behind the house and some of the sentences she caught filled her with a sense of foreboding. In spite of the sun and the scent of the hay which her husband had just brought home on the wagon, a cold dread clenched her heart and left everything all about in shadows.

It was the tale of a black-haired woman who had been hanged at the cross-roads for witchcraft, with a flaxen-haired child, the fatherless daughter of the witch, clinging to her lifeless feet when last she had been seen.

'And what has all this to do with me?' Klaus demanded, looking towards Josef for an explanation. With each word that Sebastian uttered he instinctively disliked the man more and could not bring himself to speak to him directly.

'Josef could also tell you a story. He's already told it to me,' went on Sebastian when, after a minute or so, Josef had not opened his mouth. 'The story of a child who spends every day in the forest and has for a companion a black-haired cat with the scars of a noose round its throat.'

Wilhemina cried out and clung to her husband s arm. 'Dear God,' she whimpered. 'It can't be true.'

'Silence, woman,' he snapped, and angrily turned to Josef, his eyes cold with rage. 'What lies have you been inventing, idle wretch? Have you nothing to do all day but laze in the forest, poaching I'll be bound?'

'Not lies, neighbour. Facts. Facts. I've seen them day after day, and I've hardly slept or lived since I first discovered them. It's not natural, I tell you. Not natural.'

There was no denying the genuinely expressed fear. Klaus dismissed him with a contemptuous glance and turned to Sebastian who seemed to be the motivator of all that was suddenly happening.

'Why do you come here? What do you want? What has any of this to do with you, a stranger to this village and unwelcome here?'

Sebastian answered with a sardonic smile. 'I've been received with such friendliness by all and sundry that I feel it my duty to try to save you from any unpleasantness.'

'If you have any sense of duty towards us, and all this is true, surely you should go with your tales to the priest, not bring them to me?'

'She's – as it were – your daughter and I felt that, as her father, you should be consulted first of all.'

'He's right, husband,' whimpered Wilhemina. 'We must do something before it becomes generally known.'

Angrily Klaus turned on her.

'And what do you suppose we must do? Tell me. What would you have me do for her that I haven't tried to do already? If she really is a witch, then the sooner she's condemned the better. And if she isn't – if all this is a trammel of lies – I'd like to know why this stranger and our neighbour are so anxious to involve us in them.'

Wilhemina drew back blankly from his impassively angry tone, afraid to say another word.

'Well,' went on Klaus, grimly confronting Sebastian. 'Finish what you came here to say.'

Unperturbed, Sebastian continued.

'Within a few days I intend to return to what's left of my village. I've lost everything there. Home, animals, crops. The fields are still there but the harvests are burned and trampled. The winter is before us. If I could take back a cow, perhaps, and a few chickens and even a little seed corn, I'd be in a better position to face it.' He smiled apologetically and added, 'I'm not a greedy man. I only want what is fair.'

Klaus turned his gaze to Josef. 'And you, what do you want, neighbour? My other cow? The rest of my poultry? Speak!'

'I only want to be left in peace. I didn't ask for any of this to happen. It's none of my fault. I swear it isn't.'

Josef saw that he was trapped, saw too late how Sebastian had used him and he knew that it was all the fault of that child who had cursed him. She was a witch, like her mother before her, and in his renewed misery he longed to bare his soul before God, to save himself from the hellfire that surely awaited him. His wretched expression was too natural to be doubted and it was this, rather than the stranger's threats, that disturbed Klaus.

'Run to the priest, neighbour, and confess your sins. And keep away from bad company in future,' he suggested scornfully. 'As for you, stranger,' he went on, grabbing the pitchfork that stuck out from the hay, 'the sooner you leave this village the better. There's no room here for trouble-makers.'

'Fool!' spat the man. 'But on your own head be it,' and he turned to follow the scurrying Josef, his nonchalant gait disguising his burning anger.

Fifteen

When the two men had gone Klaus stood as if paralysed. Wilhemina watched him, overtaken by a suffocating fear which his immobility and silence increased as she wondered what his next words or action might be.

'Husband,' she ventured at last when, after what seemed an endless time, he still neither moved nor spoke. 'What are you going to do?'

He turned slowly to stare at her and instead of the anger she had expected to find there was an unusual bewilderment in his eyes. He shook his head very slowly, as if trying to wake from a dream, and at last he said, 'Josef was telling the truth. He has seen something that has frightened him.'

'Josef spends his days half-drunk. You could see he was in that man's power.'

'No.' Again the slow movement of the head. 'I, too, saw something that frightened me, the night you were looking for Agnes and she didn't come. She was out here, near the pond, with some black creature in her arms. I could have sworn I heard some kind of voice.'

'You had been drinking,' she reminded him. 'You saw and heard nothing.'

'Why try to defend her? Must we lie to each other as well as to everyone else? Can't you see what she's done to us? Destroyed our lives.'

'We were already destroyed before she came to us,' Wilhemina reminded him. 'She gave me happiness for a while. Even now she sometimes gives me joy. Especially now, perhaps.'

Ignoring the irritable expression that always overcame him whenever she began to speak of the child, she rushed on, 'I've been wanting to talk to you about her, Klaus. She's different now. There's been some change in her – '

'Change! My God, how blind and foolish can a woman be! You've heard this Sebastian and our neighbour speak and you can talk of change in that hopeful tone! Mother of God, she has indeed bewitched you!' and he pressed his work-swollen hands to his head with a tortured expression.

'Klaus, Klaus,' the woman pleaded, finding courage in desperation. 'Please listen to me, I beg of you.'

'Speak then. Let's see what kind of notions she's given you.'

'If you listen with your heart closed against her, if my words fall on unsympathetic ears, there's no use in speaking. You've never loved her as I have. You've never been bad to her, I know, and I accuse you of nothing. You've tolerated her, for my sake, against every instinct of your own. You've done your best for her in your own way and for that I'm grateful. But you closed your heart against her almost from the first, when you could see that she wasn't our child though I was blinded by my love for her.' She clutched his arm, willing him to understand.

'I know very little besides the housework but my heart knows how to love. In spite of everything, I've loved Agnes. I've hated her sometimes, too, and I've despaired on many occasions. But a few weeks ago something happened, something changed her. She came home like a wild animal – I remember your words – but for the first time she was behaving like a child. Like a child, Klaus, not a stranger. She had been in some mischief, or trouble, like a child and – like a child – she has some secret.'

This last he interrupted with a scornful laugh. 'Some secret! Her whole life has been a secret!'

'No, husband, not a secret. She has never had any secrets from us until a few weeks ago. She has some terrible agony inside her that makes her unable to speak. I've seen it sometimes. I've almost felt it for her. Oh, Klaus, try to understand. I don't know how to explain these things. I can only feel them. A few weeks ago something made her act like a child instead of a shadow and since then she's had a child's secret happiness inside her. I don't know why, any more than you do, but if it's that animal, as Josef swears, then that animal can't be a bad thing.'

She ignored his incredulous gaze and rushed on. 'There's been warmth in her, Klaus. She's looked at me as I've seen other children look at their mothers. She's wanted to talk to me sometimes, to tell me of her happiness. She's moved her lips and tried. No words would come but the look was there. It was a secret happiness.'

'They say it's witchcraft,' he reminded her bitterly but his voice was gentle for she had impressed him in a way that nothing ever had. Never had this wife of his spoken so many words at one time, at least never since their early days together, before all their unhappiness began. Her voice, her eyes, her whole body eloquently pleaded and he was secretly amazed at this vision of a woman he had never known.

'Witchcraft?' she answered him. 'Can happiness be caused by witchcraft?'

'I don't know, wife. I don't know.'

'Surely there can be good witchcraft sometimes?'

Klaus moved his head in the same bewildered way as

before. He drew closer to the woman and put his arm round her shoulders, feeling an unusual warmth towards her. For so long she had hardly been more to him than his cows and his fields and his implements that he was almost overwhelmed by the discovery that she could still mean something to him.

'They burned all the cats in the village. I remember my father talking about it. I suppose some could have survived in the forest, but no one has ever seen them.'

'Surely cats are animals, the same as our beasts?'

'I don't know, wife. People have always been afraid of them. They are not like other animals.'

They were silent for a while then Klaus said, 'I went to the forest several times to look for her mother. Someone should have been there. I should have found a body.'

'Someone abandoned her and ran away.'

'There were no signs, not even of the child herself, except for a scrap of her dress caught on a bush. No footprints. Nothing.'

'The leaves could have covered them. It was autumn.'

'If she is that woman's child – the one they hanged. . . .'

'Do you really think she may be, husband?'

'I don't know. The story that man told us hangs together well. Could she have wandered so far on her own and escaped the boars and the wolves, let alone the hunger she must have endured?'

Again they were silent, Klaus recalling the years he had suffered the child's presence, remembering more than anything else her uncannily empty eyes, the gaze that seemed to see all and yet nothing, the pain she never felt, her complete and utter non-existence, non-participation among them. And Wilhemina was telling herself that she was not mistaken. Agnes was beginning to come alive after so many years of soullessness. She would fight to the death, if necessary, to preserve that first childish happiness she had seen in her, regardless of witchcraft, regardless even of God if so it must be.

She clenched her husband's hand instinctively and he returned the action. She began to cry and he stroked her head in an effort to comfort her.

'What are we going to do?' she asked him. 'What are we going to do?'

Sixteen

'I must find the cat and kill it.'

This statement was uttered by Klaus after he had spent the next hour unloading hay from the wagon.

'Kill it!'

'Let us suppose that Josef and that man are telling the truth, that the cat is some kind of a witch, the child's mother reincarnated – God knows what it represents. I don't understand it myself. But if you want me to save Agnes for you some way or another, the cat must be destroyed.'

Wilhemina's eyes gazed at him with cold clarity.

'I can promise you, husband, that if you kill the cat you will kill her.'

'Why do you say that? What do you know that you haven't told me? For God's sake, woman, this is no time to remain silent. Tell me all you know, once and for all.'

'I only know what my heart tells me. The stranger has told us an unusual story which may, or may not, be true. We both know that Agnes has the cat. You saw her with it that night. I bathed the scratches on her arms. But you didn't see the look in her eyes and you haven't noticed the change in her these last few weeks. It's a change for the good I tell you, husband. And the cause of the change has been the cat. If you kill the cat, you'll kill her.'

'And if I don't kill the cat? Where do you suppose Josef is now? And that man Sebastian? Do you think he has no more tricks up his sleeve? What's going to happen when the whole village gets to hear about it? You heard his story. You heard how they treated that poor devil of her mother – '

'If it was her mother,' broke in Wilhemina.

'Mother or not, witch or not, no one asks questions that require any answers in such moments. Do you want to see our home burned down, do you want us tortured and murdered? Do you want to see Agnes tortured and murdered too?'

The look of unbelieving horror that dawned in her expression as he spoke filled him with pity.

'Understand something, wife. If Agnes is taken and found guilty of witchcraft, she will be tortured and put to death. What matter that she's only a child? A witch isn't a human being. She has no soul or Christian feelings. There will be no one to pity her or to pity us. And we don't even know, anyway, whether it's true. Perhaps she is a witch and she's been using us all these years.'

'Never. Never. I'll never believe she's a witch.'

'Well, be that as it may, I must act quickly if you want me to save her and all of us. So far it's only Josef's word against ours.'

'And the other man?'

'If I can destroy the proof his words won't matter. He's a stranger here and a rogue. The only proof is the cat, wife. You can see that, surely?'

She nodded slowly.

'If there's no cat nothing Josef says can have any value,' he insisted. 'She's always been strange. People are used to her. They'll say Josef was drunk and that the other man used him for his own interest. My word will always be respected above his.'

He waited for her to say something. He expected her to agree. At last she looked at him and spoke, but only to affirm what she had already said.

'When you kill the cat Agnes will die.'

'And will it matter so very much?'

'I don't know, husband, but if you kill the cat you will be murdering her.'

'What else can I do then?' he shouted at her, almost ready to strike her for her stubborn insistence. 'I'm willing to risk my immortal soul for her. What else can you ask of a man?'

'You could give Sebastian the cow and the poultry and some seed corn. Then he would go away and not trouble us again.'

'And Josef, what about him? He's probably gabbling away to the priest at this minute.'

'Your word is stronger than Josef's. Give the stranger our cow. Give him what he asks for and send him away.'

'And afterwards?'

'Afterwards?'

'Yes. Afterwards. What are we going to do about Agnes and the cat?'

'Leave her. Let her nurse it in the woods. Let her feed it. Let her try to talk to it. Each day I see her happier. Each day there's more of the child in her expression. Each night she whimpers less and each morning she wakes with greater inner joyfulness. Klaus, Klaus. Do it for me.'

She clung to his arm, all the agony of the long, fruitless years expressed in her eyes.

At that moment Klaus was tempted to yield to her. They had known so little pleasure. There had always been so much hardship. She had asked him for so few things and he had given her nothing but a share in his toil and dreariness. But again the memory of the child's gaze stabbed like a shaft through his being and a true fear suddenly clutched at him.

If she really were a witch she would be capable of

allying Wilhemina to her cause. Perhaps the change she had seen had been no more than a satanic power within Agnes which blinded her to the truth. Was that power working strongly now, giving Wilhemina words that never in her life had she been capable of uttering, giving her the power to plead that had stirred him to the heart, giving her this strength and wisdom that he had never seen?

'No, no,' he suddenly cried. 'It cannot be. I admit I don't understand her. I admit I've never even sought very far. I admit that in your love for her you may have seen and felt things that were lost on me. But I cannot pretend that none of this has happened. I cannot give a stranger the fruits of my toil to silence perhaps God's truth, even though He should choose a vile way to reveal it. If she's a witch, Wilhemina, she must be destroyed before she destroys us all. Have you forgotten that we're only mortal, that one day we must stand before God in the Final Judgement?'

He took control of himself before finally adding, 'If that cat has power over Agnes its death can only release her from it. If Agnes is a witch and the cat's death will be hers too, then it will be a blessing for us all.'

'And if she's only a child, husband? If she's only a child and the cat is only a cat?'

'Then may God have mercy on us all. I can only do as my conscience bids me.'

*

Wilhemina watched while he sharpened a stave to a point, put a knife and an axe in his belt, recited the Lord's Prayer and crossed himself.

The sun was still warm over the fields. There remained a couple of hours of full daylight at least before sunset. It would be darker in the forest but not too dark for him to see sufficiently well to complete the task he had set himself. He had two hours in which to find Agnes and destroy the first happiness of her short life and, as he was a conscientious man in all that he did, Wilhemina knew he would be successful.

As soon as he was gone, she took a bowl of curds covered her face with her shawl and hurried to her own secret place where she had often prayed in the past. Klaus was going, as he believed, to do God's work. She must call on different spirits if, somehow, Agnes's soul was to be saved.

Seventeen

There were many narrow footpaths in the forest, mostly on its outskirts where the villagers came to collect the brushwood and fallen branches which were theirs by right, but only a few that led into its depths. Klaus was law-abiding by nature, believing that every man should remain within his allotted span, finding contentment if he could and if not enduring whatever God saw fit to send him, and he endeavoured to keep within the law, down to its smallest detail. The law said that the forest belonged to the baron and the footpaths were private and, therefore, denied to him.

He had broken the law before when he had gone to look for some clue to Agnes's appearance among them. He had searched for hours for a body or a recent fire and had found only a scrap of home-spun clinging to a holly bush. Which path should he take now to find the child herself and her uncanny companion?

While he stood hesitating, a stocky man with a zeal for complying with duty however distasteful that duty might be, but with a heart that stirred in pity for his wife who had begged him to ignore duty for love, he saw that the hard-beaten paths were damp from the earlier showers of the week. He could make out the thin forked lines of birds' feet and the deeper smudges that might represent the passing of a rabbit, and so be began to look for a human footprint which might lead him to Agnes.

He did not find any naked toe-marks to guide him but

he did discover the deeper imprints of the rough boots of Josef and Sebastian. He gripped his stake more firmly and began to follow them, only aware that he had left the outskirts far behind by the growing darkness all about him and the numerous thick trunks whose foliage hardly gave a glimpse of the sky. He became aware of a greater silence, broken only by his heavy tread and the occasional jabber of a bird or squirrel. The forest was cool and damp, and seemed to cling to him. Had he come for a different purpose he might have sensed its soothing influence. As it was, a shiver ran down his spine.

After a while, still following the blurred imprints, he grew aware of a change in the light. There was an open space ahead of him where the sun's rays gleamed as they filtered through the ferns and branches. Instinctively his pace slowed. Would he come upon the child at last?

As he drew slowly closer he became aware of the slight figure in the evening sunlight. He could not yet tell that it was Agnes but he knew that it could be no other. Near the edge of the glade were some bushes. Perhaps Josef and his companion had concealed themselves in that very spot to spy on her! He too drew himself up in that place, hardly breathing, not knowing what he might see.

He breathed in sharply when he caught his first full glimpse of the child. There was an uncanny beauty in her that he had never seen before. Perhaps it was the sheer delight registered in her eyes and on her open lips or the sense of liberty expressed in every movement of her limbs. He had never seen her like this before, shining with rare brilliance, and had it not been that a darker reason had brought him here, with an axe, a knife and a stake, he might have believed her to be inspired by God, such was the impression of grace and innocence she imparted.

Where were those cold, deathlike eyes whose expression had killed every spontaneous feeling he might have had for her? What had become of that limp, unfeeling, unapproachable body that had hardly any contact with the material world, belonging nowhere and often seeming not to exist?

This creature was alive and warm, intensely real, and at first sight Klaus's heart filled with pain as he choked back an involuntary cry of amazement. This was how Agnes should always have been. Like this he would have loved her and devoted all his efforts to her well-being. Had Wilhemina ever seen her like this? Was this what she meant by a change in her? What had happened? Was she two people inside the one frame?

It took only seconds to feel all this – for they were feelings rather than thoughts that possessed him at that moment – and even as the painful question formed inside him, he became aware of the black thing that possessed all the child's attention. Cavorting, twisting, rolling, grabbing at its tail with outstretched claws, its movements both graceful yet serpent-like, it drew the man's breathless attention from the child with insidious force, and all that was forthright and good in him revolted against the primitive, hypnotic power of the cat's movements.

It was the only cat he had ever seen, although he had heard tell of them. He had seen a picture of one in a book brought by a pedlar when, in curiosity, he had handed over a coin for the privilege of opening its pages and staring at the black and grey drawings of witches, angels, and devils' cauldrons. That had been many years ago but the things he had seen on those pages had so impressed him that they had never left his memory. Now and again he would think of them. His vision of hell came more from his memory of the pictures than from all the priest's sermons. He recalled the grimaces of pain in the people's

faces, their jaws stretched wide in agony, and the relentless satisfaction in the Devil's glance when they pleaded in vain for mercy. And he remembered the cat, walking on its hind legs, its expression diabolically human as it watched its mistress, a witch with goat's head and wings, roast a small naked child over some flames.

His memory of the pictures was confused though vivid. There had been angels and saints in the book as well as devils and witches but the pictures had been so new and startling an experience that he hardly recalled them in proper sequence. He remembered only the horror they had inspired and now, before his eyes, was the only cat he had ever seen, attended with slave-like devotion by this astoundingly different child to whom he had given his daughter's name but whom he had never ever known.

Klaus was too sick with disgust to feel any fear at that moment. What had caused Josef to recoil with dread brought his righteous blood to immediate boiling point. He sprang out from his hiding place with a hideous cry of rage, aware of nothing but the cat which immediately stopped its movements, stretching its neck to look at him in startled surprise before, a second later, dashing towards the trees on the farther side of the glade.

Klaus's first grab did not reach it but his second caught a handful of tail to which he held with all his might. The cat yowled fearfully, adding to the man's convinced impression of its diabolical properties, and even as he held it up, knife in hand, intently seeking the place in which to plunge it, he caught sight of Agnes's agonized expression.

It was only half a second – half a second in which all her joy, beauty and brightness fled. She reached out her arms in his direction, her mouth open as if she would

speak. He struck with his knife. The cat screeched then somehow curled up on itself and sank its teeth into his hand. Gasping with pain, he struck again, and this time it was the child who cried out in agony.

'Agnes!' she cried, 'Agnes,' and collapsed in the grass.

The cat was running away, body close to the ground, bleeding but free. Klaus had dropped his knife and was holding his wrist, watching blood pulse from the wounds the cat's teeth had inflicted, terrified that he would be possessed by madness. And then he saw the child, senseless on the ground, and remembered how she had cried out the only human word she had ever uttered in his presence. Agnes. Agnes. Her name. Why had she cried that word above all others? What force had suddenly given her speech?

He found himself shaking with cold, although his whole body was clammy with perspiration. He saw the blood on his knife and dug the blade into the earth to clean it. Blood no longer welled from the punctures in his hand but it was already puffy and painful and tinged with purple. He stared at the wounds but took a grip of his fear, ashamed to be as weak as Josef.

Darkness was falling quickly now. The sun was almost gone and he must find his way back along the once-trodden paths with little or no light to guide him. It was no good looking for the cat. Perhaps it would die from the knife thrusts, although if it were a witch in animal form there would be little chance of that. And what about the child? What should he do with her?

He went over to her and knelt down beside her. She was quite unconscious, all colour fled from the cheeks which looked suddenly sunken and almost grey. An awful thought struck him. He put his ear against her chest to listen for heartbeats. No, she was not dead.

A memory flashed through his head at that moment,

of the first Agnes who had lain as pale and still in her cot in the grey light of a winter's morning – how many years ago? For the first time since then he gave way to the pain that unexpectedly seared him at the time-worn memory. One broken sob escaped him. Then he gathered the unconscious child in his arms and went back home with her.

Eighteen

He could see the turmoil in the village as he approached across the fields. Josef or Sebastian must have spoken. In the fast-gathering gloom he could make out the figures of his neighbours, their greys and browns and greens fused into one sunset colouring. Their voices were high and excited. Light sprang from their lanterns and torches as they forgathered at the church.

Luckily his own dwelling was on the outskirts and he could reach it without having to pass them by. For once he felt scorn for his neighbours, working themselves to such a pitch at the words of idle Josef and the stranger. At the same time a new fear struck him. Although he himself had warned his wife what to expect from an enraged and frightened crowd, he had spoken from hearsay, not experience, and this first glimpse of people not yet well warmed to their task but undoubtedly eager, sent a chill to the pit of his stomach which gave extra speed to his weary body.

The child's weight was nothing to him as he crossed the remaining distance to his home, coming the back way, behind the pond, for the first time sneaking like a thief to his own property. Wilhemina was waiting in the doorway for him. She had returned from her own pilgrimage much earlier and on hearing the rising noise in the streets had grown anxious for her man who tarried so and the child he had gone to seek.

But her very anxiety gave her strength just as Klaus's was about to fail him. She almost dragged the child from his arms and laid her in the cot, hurriedly throwing a blanket over her, asking as she did so, 'Your hand? What have you done to your hand?'

'The cat. It bit me. I'm afraid, wife. I'm afraid.'

'Ssh! There's no time for fear. I'm sure the priest will be here any minute. We can't let him see that hand.'

As she spoke she was examining the wounds, Klaus watching with bewilderment, wondering where she suddenly found her strength and determination. At that moment he was incapable of thought, too much affected by recent events and convinced of the child's malevolent power. He scorned his neighbours for listening to Josef but knew that, had they seen what he had seen, there would be no hope of saving Agnes.

'This is going to hurt but it's the only thing I can think of,' Wilhemina was saying. 'Those wounds must be cauterized before the poison sets in.'

She led him to the fireplace where a black cauldron sat on an iron over a low flame. She removed the pot and told her husband to kneel in front of the fire.

'Put you hand in the flame,' she commanded. 'It will sear all the flesh and cure it. At the same time it will disguise the cat's teethmarks.'

Klaus hesitated, thinking of the pain that the dancing flame would inflict.

'Be quick,' Wilhemina insisted. 'There's no time to lose.' She grabbed his arm as she spoke and held it for a few seconds over the fire, resisting her husband's automatic reaction and his yell of pain.

'There,' she cried. 'It's done,' and she hurried to find a clean cloth in which to bind it, leaving Klaus half fainting beside the fireplace.

Just then began an impatient knocking. She took no notice but went on with her task of binding the injured hand. The door flew open and several men pushed their way in, followed by the priest with dark, implacable expression.

'What do you want? What do you want?' cried Wilhemina. 'Is this the way to burst into a Christian home?'

'What's going on here?' the priest answered, motioning the men to one side, taking in at a glance Klaus's deathly features, the hand half-bandaged, the woman's wild expression and the child either asleep or unconscious in the cot.

Without waiting for an answer he went over to the cot and pulled back the covering, his lips tightening at the sight of her fully clothed body. Again he turned back to Klaus and Wilhemina and repeated his question, pointedly raising his glance from the child.

Klaus was in no condition to think quickly but Wilhemina was as if inspired that night. It frightened him to see how much she was mistress of herself in such a dangerous situation. Where had such self-control come from? He sank back against the wall with a groan, overcome by his thoughts and fear as well as by pain.

'Agnes tripped and would have fallen into the fire had not my husband thrown her to one side. She fell so heavily that she lost her senses. At the same time my husband lost his balance as he pushed her and his hand went into the flames.'

'Let me see,' said the priest.

'I was just binding it up when you came. I haven't even had time to see to the child, except to put her into bed as you found her.'

The priest removed the bandage, unimpeded by Klaus who had nothing to say for himself. He stared at the blistering and broken flesh, then bound it up again. Afterwards he went back to Agnes and looked down at her.

'How long has she been like this?'

'A few minutes, that's all. It's only just happened.'

'Where has she been all day?'

Wilhemina raised her hands in a helpless gesture. 'You know what she is, Father. Never at home. She plays here and there and comes back when she's hungry.'

'I suppose you are aware of Josef's accusations.'

'He came here with a stranger who tried to force my husband into giving him a cow and some of our poultry.'

'And why should he want to do that? What hold has he over your husband? Speak, Klaus. All this very much concerns you.'

Klaus unsteadily rose to his feet and went to sit on the bench at the table. He leaned his elbows on the board, watched by many pairs of eyes for those that had not managed to enter with the priest were crowding the doorway, determined to miss as little of the events as possible.

'I don't know what you're all doing here in my house. Why so much noise? Why so much scandal? Can't a man be at peace in his own home?'

'Not when he's sheltering a witch,' someone shouted back at him and there was a murmur of approval all round.

Klaus did not know what to answer. In his own heart he believed the accusation because of what he had seen but his innate sense of justice instinctively rose against these interfering neighbours who had seen nothing but automatically accused, ready to tear apart his wife's little world on the basis of a few spoken words.

The priest took a seat at the head of the table, on the man's left, and sensing his turmoil without knowing the genuine reason for it – was it only for the shock of burning his hand? – with greater restraint said, 'Tell me what has happened, Klaus. You're an honest man and I shall believe anything you tell me.'

'No!' cried Wilhemina, throwing herself between them. 'You've come here believing Josef's accusations and the words of a stranger. They're lies. Lies. They only wanted our cow and poultry. Tell them, Klaus. Tell them how it was.'

Klaus felt the priest's sharp eyes boring into him and he lifted his own to meet them. His stare was of such intensity that the priest instinctively knew that when this man spoke he would speak the truth regardless of the consequences. It was not what Josef or the stranger might say, but Klaus's own words which would either confirm or clear the accusation that had been brought against the child.

Nineteen

'She spoke,' he said. 'I have never heard her voice before. Seven years has she lived under my roof and tonight I heard her speak for the first time.'

'Klaus!' exclaimed his wife. Everyone else was silent.

'She cried out, "Agnes! Agnes!" '

'Her own name?' queried the priest.

'My daughter's name. She died when she was three.'

'What are you trying to say?' the priest asked him.

Klaus slowly shook his head. 'I don't know. I only know what I heard. She cried out, "Agnes, Agnes", and then she lost her senses.'

'Where was this? Here in this room?'

'In the forest. We were in the forest. I had gone to look for her.'

'Had you gone because of what Josef had said?'

'I went to fulfil a duty.'

'What duty? You must tell me,' the priest insisted.

In spite of his admonition Klaus seemed unwilling to say any more. Wilhemina had gone to the child's cot and was leaning over her, stroking the pallid forehead. Her reddened cheeks glistened with tears and she was heard to murmur, 'My little Agnes. I have prayed for you. I have prayed.'

'What happened in the forest?' the priest went on. 'Was she alone?'

The man's blue eyes met his own and his voice was bitter, though subdued, as he answered, 'She has always been alone. She has never been anything but alone.'

'But was there anyone – or anything – else in the forest besides yourself and her? Who did she cry out to? And why the name?'

'In the forest I saw a black creature that held her in its sway. She was different while the creature was there . . .' He hesitated, remembering, looking for words. 'She was lovely. For the first time she was Agnes.'

'Explain yourself clearly. Who do you refer to when you talk of Agnes? Your own child or this, this – '

'This what?' Klaus suddenly snapped at him. 'You baptized her. You gave her the name. My wife called her Agnes and loved her like a daughter. But until tonight she has never been Agnes to me. My daughter was buried years ago and this – this changeling was no more than an intruder that couldn't even speak.'

The last words were scornful, bitter, but his voice changed as he went on, 'But for the first time, tonight, I saw her as a child. She looked like an angel until I held the cat and thrust my knife into it. It was then that she screamed out "Agnes, Agnes" and fell to the ground. But the thing I brought back home – that creature there,' he jerked his head in the direction of the cot where Wilhemina, the tears coursing freely though noiselessly down her cheeks, stroked the child's head in ferocious devotion, 'is not my daughter and never can be.'

The listening neighbours looked from one to another. They had come without knowing what to expect, what to find or hear, but never would they have imagined hearing the words Klaus had just pronounced. They had expected denials, excuses or even a confession, but what they had heard was beyond their understanding.

There was witchcraft of a kind, of that there could be no doubt, but on whom to lay the blame and how to extirpate it, they had no idea. This talk of two different Agneses, one that was and one that was not and by whom even honest Klaus was deceived, filled them with genuine fear. The priest had asked, To whom had the child cried? No one could answer, except perhaps Agnes herself who lay unconscious. And why was she unconscious now? Had the spirit that had moved her all these years suddenly fled?

Each one puzzled in his slow, deliberate way. Their burning zeal to hunt out the witch among them had gone, to be replaced by the darkest fear of things not understood, and even the priest looked at Klaus wonderingly, trying to gauge the depth of his honesty and wondering whether he was deliberately trying to confuse them. But no. It was obvious to all that he was equally confused.

What was the relationship between the two children, the cat, and the woman who had disappeared off the scaffold in that other village after being hanged for witchcraft?

'You realize we must take the child away?' he said at last, still not knowing how this would affect Klaus.

'What are you going to do with her?' screamed Wilhemina with tortured voice, still clinging to the unconscious child.

'She must be watched and the truth must be discovered.'

'Klaus. Klaus. Don't let them take her away.'

She ran to him and fell on her knees beside him, her hands grasping his arm. He did not even look at her as he answered, 'They must do as they think fit.'

'She's ill. She's very ill. I think she may die. I told you what would happen if you killed the cat.'

'What did you tell him?' the priest demanded, wondering whether this woman might know more than her husband.

'I told him what none of you can see. That she's a child who found a cat in the forest and gave it her love because for one reason or another she could never give her love to us. She wanted something to love, the same as all of us, but she couldn't speak and perhaps that's why she came to love something that couldn't speak either.'

'You're blinded by affection,' the priest told her. 'If it were not for that you yourself would see that none of this is natural.'

'She's lived among us all for seven years and no one has ever accused her of witchcraft. It was only that man Sebastian, coming here with his tales to get something out of us for what he has lost, who has brought all this misfortune upon us.'

'Silence,' the priest commanded, for her voice rose hysterically and her actions were wild. 'I myself, in this very room, not long ago reminded both of you that God is not mocked. Perhaps now you will see the truth of those words.'

He stood up and signalled to one of his followers to take the child. Wilhemina rushed to the cot and protectively guarded it with her body.

'No, no,' she cried. 'I'll not let you take her.'

'She will be observed without prejudice and when she regains consciousness, assuming that so it will be, she will be tried with all justice.'

'How can she defend herself without words? Her own silence must condemn her.'

'If she's innocent God will find a way of enlightening her and us. Have faith, woman,' the priest sternly adjured, and he nodded again to the man nearest the cot.

Wilhemina wildly took hold of him, dragging on his arms, until she was pulled roughly aside by another and held struggling, and wailing desperately, while a third took the child in his arms, wrapping the covering about her as he hastily abandoned the room. The long fair hair and the dirty, naked toes were all that could be seen of her. As soon as they had gone the man who held Wilhe-mina pushed her down to the bench beside her husband and hurried after his companions, slamming the door behind him.

Klaus put a restraining arm on his wife, for she was about to race after them, and she fell back beside him, throwing herself across the table to weep loud and desperately, but to no avail.

Twenty

All that long, miserable night Klaus and Wilhemina lay awake. Since Agnes had been taken from them not a word was exchanged between them. Klaus had made no effort to console his distracted wife and when at last she could weep no more she had gone about her tasks as though this night were the same as all the rest.

For a long time he had watched her, nursing his aching hand, too stunned by the torrent of events to think of anything to say. At length he began to reflect on what had happened. He went on watching Wilhemina, even while he thought, and understood instinctively that if anything happened to the child now she would be utterly destroyed.

If the death of their own child had benumbed their love at least there had been sufficient feeling to make their life together bearable, if only in that they shared the same great sorrow. He realized now that he had never understood how much she had needed this second child, even though she had sometimes almost hated her. In spite of everything there had been a link of love, one-sided perhaps, and he, Klaus, had wrought the blow that had severed the link, destroying everything in his effort to be honest.

He argued with himself, needing to be assured. She had not seen what he had seen. She had blinded herself so long to the child's defects and strangeness that she refused to see things clearly as he did, as clearly as everyone else in the village would see them. Sebastian was a rogue and there might be little truth in his story, Josef was an untrustworthy idler, but no unprejudiced person could deny that the things he had seen were beyond any natural explanation.

While he watched his wife he had to wonder if she had all along known the child's true nature. He was still astounded by her sudden ability to defend her so powerfully, almost to persuade him of the truth of her convictions. Josef's revelations had not seemed to astound her. She had been frightened, he remembered that, but it might have been fear that at last she was discovered. How could she understand the child so well when he himself had never got beyond the barrier of her soulless stare?

As he asked himself these unanswerable questions over and over again, convinced that he was right but agonizingly aware of the error he might be making which would destroy all three of them if it could not be put right, calmness once again deserted him. He could not utter a single word to that isolated, tortured soul that shared the house with him that night and throughout the darkness he groaned and sighed and moved impatiently, longing for the dawn so that he could return to his fields and lose himself in his tasks.

He was haunted by the memory of the child s face, that joyful, open expression which he seemed to remember as a halo about her and which even now caught at his heart with pain. Why should he have seen that expression only once in all these years? He would have loved her, he knew he would have loved her, if only once she had looked at him in that way.

The morning came at last. He went off to his fields with his tools, determined not to think of the child until the priest should send him word, and he was glad to be out so early, before everyone else, so that he could avoid the gossip that was sure to be rife that day.

Wilhemina, too, had been thinking all night. She did not think in her husband's way, trying to reason the right or wrong of the case. She reasoned with her heart and her heart was bitterly wounded, aching with the persistence of an immense physical pain. If sometimes she had doubted her love for the child, wearied by constant rejection, she knew now that she loved this second Agnes more than the first.

She could not even remember that first child, seeing only the face of the second, recalling only the expression of need that she had sometimes understood. She could only remember when she had held her struggling in her arms, howling and sobbing, tormented by fears she could never name, by a sadness she could never pronounce, and the look she would direct at her before succumbing to exhaustion. Agnes had loved her in those moments although she could never say so.

She knew that Agnes had wanted to tell her about the cat. It was only because she could not speak that Josef and Sebastian had been able to twist and turn her most innocent actions into something wicked. It was always men that spoke of witchcraft. Were they so afraid of love? Love had touched her heart at last, had filtered through that impenetrable barrier which she herself had never been able to pass, and she knew that only the continuation of that love could save Agnes from destruction.

She did not understand what kind of destruction implacably awaited her. She only knew by instinct something she could never explain with words. It was true that sometimes it had seemed she was in the Devil's grasp, when in a sudden flash of inexplicable violence she would throw down and try to break everything within her reach, but those moments were always followed by the tears and clinging need which had made Wilhemina love her in spite of everything, renewing hope when hope was almost gone.

The cat was making her different, bringing warmth to her frozen heart, light to her lightless eyes, peace to her tormented imagination, and while she remembered – completely isolated from the man who lay beside her in the bed, unaware of his tossings and sighings – she burned with determination to save her somehow, regardless of what men might say, regardless even of the Devil.

Only the cat could save her. Klaus did not say he had killed it. It had bitten him and run away. The chances were that it was still in the forest, injured but alive. If only the dawn would come soon! How many hours must pass before she could do something for Agnes, and she

passed from despair to hope, from fear to impatience, longing for the sunrise.

*

No sooner was Klaus out of sight than she too set off on a mission of her own. It was to her advantage, also, that they had both risen before any of their neighbours. The village was still slumbering. The mist was thick, promising a day of heat, and the sun glowed almost the colour of blood through the grey dawn.

Wilhemina's heart beat fast with fear and hope as she set off towards the forest, a closed basket on her arm under her shawl, with which she almost completely shrouded her face, until the village was left well behind. When she reached the edge of the trees she looked back but there was no one in the fields, which were just beginning to gleam with sunlight. She looked for her husband but could not see him. Luckily his strips of land were on the far side of the river, hardly visible beneath the bank of mist.

The forest too seemed dark and grey. She felt spiders webs across her face as she passed between the trees whose trunks were marked with silvery slime. Everything was damp and the all-prevading silence of the forest's morning stillness caused her to halt involuntarily. She stood unmoving, grasping her shawl beneath her chin and shivering, and then she heard the birds, some a long way off, some closer, and when they began to call and answer, the tall, dark arches of trees, growing so closely from between the wilderness of ferns and bushes, no longer inspired her with fear.

Unknowingly repeating her husband's actions of the previous evening, she examined the different footpaths until the marks in the soil gave her a clue as to the direction she must choose. Had it not been for her love and determination she might have been afraid to plunge into that forbidding wilderness, but once she knew she was on the right track all fear left her.

She came to the glade where Agnes had played and here, at its edges, the tracks she had followed abruptly ended. So this had been the scene of her joy, this grassy place so empty and silent, which the sun was just beginning to pierce as its rays broke in thin lines through the heavy summer foliage! There was no sign that she had ever been there except – except for that rust-red smattering on the grass blades which had resisted the morning dew.

Where had the stricken creature fled? Had it died in the undergrowth or was it nursing its wounds not far from here, awaiting the child's return? Was it watching her now, malevolently perhaps, thinking that she, too, wished it ill?

Now that she was so close to the cat's domain a new fear caught at her heart. Until that moment she had hardly considered the cat, except in its relation to Agnes. What if it really were a witch or had magical powers? What if her husband were right? What if she were meddling in things beyond her understanding which only her love for Agnes made her ignore? All these doubts flashed through her head in an instant but she knew there was no going back without completing her task.

Where to? Where to? Where could she look in the immensity of the forest all about her? There was a trail of blood across the grass which led her to a tangle of impenetrable undergrowth. Was the animal somewhere within that mass of bramble, bush and wiry grass? If so, she would never be able to find it.

Almost despairing, she wandered back and forth, pushing her shawl off her head for by now the sun was giving more warmth. And then she saw the tree with its hollow and her heart instinctively leaped. There was the place! She was sure of it. Why had she not seen it before?

Cautiously, with fear in her heart, she approached the tree, noticing the grass flecked with bloodstains round about. It was a brighter colour than that rusty red she had first seen. Perhaps it was fresher. Hardly breathing, she knelt down when she reached the tree, put her basket to one side and carefully peered in. The hollow was large and deep and its darkness was such that her own shadow made it impossible for her to see anything.

The memory of the terrible bite on her husband's hand kept her from taking any risks but she moved her body and again tried to see into the dark interior. Was it her imagination or was there a darker shape amid the darkness, far back hardly within her reach?

She rose and went to look for a stick, thinking to prod about with it and thus discover the truth without incurring any bites, and sure enough the stick told her what she wanted to know when it came up against something soft and yielding. The animal was there. Was it still alive? Was it dangerous?

Cautiously she prodded again, sensing the same softness, but aware of no movement. And then she did gather all her courage, reaching into the hollow with both hands, dragging out the unresisting body to the light of day.

Twenty-one

With wildfire speed the news of the night's happenings passed through the village. Josef and Sebastian were besieged on every side by questioners, some incredulous, some willing to believe and insisting that it was only to be supposed that such a thing would happen sooner or later, everyone morbidly interested. They collected in groups outside the church and meeting house, hopeful of seeing the child, determined to hear the priest's opinion just as soon as he should make an appearance, and all Sebastian's neighbours found themselves equally mobbed, with demands on every side to tell what they knew of their witch and her daughter.

'And where is Klaus? And where's his wife?' they began to demand.

No one could recall having seen them that day. Had they been taken into custody, too? Were they all locked up together? The men who had carried Agnes away gave their version of the story and each time it was repeated, it was changed and exaggerated so that by mid-morning there were a dozen different tales flying from mouth to mouth.

Women were suddenly afraid for their children, men were equally worried about their crops and animals. Would the child be capable of cursing them? And what of the cat? Was it beast or devil? And where was it hidden? Klaus, working stolidly and unthinkingly in his fields, refusing that morning to think of anything but the task in front of him, found himself dragged back to the village by a crowd of men who came in search of him. They shouted questions at him, they jostled him unnecessarily, and rage and fear equally choked him.

As for Wilhemina, where was she? They had gone to her house but it was deserted. They had thrown the furniture aside, seeking for signs of witchcraft while not really knowing what they were looking for. The slightest suspicious thing would have served them but there was nothing in that house that could not be found in their own, except for a collection of smooth stones in a box together with a few dried berries and leaves that fell to powder when they were touched.

They thrust the box in Klaus's face and demanded to know what this odd collection meant. He would answer none of their questions, nor retaliate to any of their insults or insinuations, certain that whatever he said would go unheeded if not actually twisted to satisfy their insatiable demand for some sensational proof.

Everyone was recalling the child they had nearly forgotten all these years and it was now that Josef remembered how she had obliged him, just by the look in her eyes, to bring her to the village when she came from the forest all alone all those years ago. It did not seem to him that he was telling a lie. Seven years had passed. The truth was that he could remember that day but vaguely and the only things he could recall about Agnes were recent ones. It seemed the same to him – the child now and the child then – and the child now was a witch. He had proof of it with the things he had seen himself and the things Sebastian had told him.

When the priest at last appeared, after dithering for some time in his house not knowing how he should greet his parishioners that morning, everyone flocked towards him with a great cry, demanding to know the truth, demanding to be told if there was indeed a witch among them and what was to be done with her if it were so.

The priest held up his hand for silence. Klaus, caught between two men who had virtually made a prisoner of him, was equally anxious to hear his reply. His heart beat painfully and for a second he vaguely understood that silent child. If no one could understand you, what was the use of speech? Where was his wife? What had happened to her? Had something occurred since he had gone to his fields so early that day? He longed to hear the priest's words which would perhaps clarify this terrible situation.

At last the noise abated sufficiently for him to begin to speak and, as a good shepherd should, he rated his flock for its unruly behaviour. He saw Klaus with his strained expression, his arms held by a man on either side, and halted his railing with the demand that he be set free.

'How dare you take judgment into your own hands?' he shouted at the self-imposed jailers. 'How dare you presume to judge your own neighbour without rhyme or reason?'

'Where is his wife?' one of them sullenly replied. 'We've been to look for her but she's gone.'

'Listen to me, all of you,' went on the priest, without answering. 'The child is with me. I have her under observation. Accusations have been brought against her which may, or may not, be true, but which must certainly be investigated. In the meantime nothing can be served by violent behaviour and ridiculous expectation.'

'There are plenty of ways of finding out if she's a witch,' someone shouted from the back of the crowd.

'Duck her in the river,' yelled another voice. 'It's a well-known fact that witches never drown.'

The man who was looking after the box with Agnes's few treasures thrust himself forward and placed it in the priest's hands. 'Get her to explain what these things are for,' he said. 'We found them hidden beneath the firewood in her house.'

The priest lifted the lid and loud murmurings rose again while he examined the contents.

'Stones, berries, old leaves?' he said, his raised voice expressing ridicule for the doubt these harmless objects could raise. 'A child's playthings, that's all they are.'

'Tell us, Klaus. Tell us. Is she a witch? You were in the forest. Everyone knows that now. Is she a witch? Is your daughter a witch? Come on. Tell us. We want to know.'

'She's not my daughter,' he shouted. 'I gave her a home but she's not my daughter. As for whether or not she's a witch, if a few stones and berries can condemn her, God help you all.'

'Make her speak! Make her speak!' another voice demanded. 'Klaus said she spoke in the forest. If she could speak then, she can do it now, in front of all of us. We all want to hear her speak.'

A great chorus of approval rose at these words and the priest was taken aback by the crowd's excited mood. He did not know what to do. He had hardly slept all night, wondering about that speechless child, remembering Wilhemina's desperate question. How can she defend herself without words?

Who would speak for her at a trial? Was it enough to rely on God's judgment? Would God really intercede for her if she were innocent or, at least, would the sign He gave be sufficiently obvious for them to understand?

He realized that his doubts were heresy but he had never come across such a strange child in his lifetime and Klaus, for all his honesty, seemed confused and uncertain. Was he to believe Josef, a noted idler and good-for-nothing? Was he to believe Sebastian, an outsider who had only revealed his story after failing to make Klaus pay for his silence?

And what would the villagers believe? They were all equally afraid of Agnes because she was different. Some of them were jealous of Klaus because fortune had smiled on him, at least in regard to his land and animals, and for the same reason many women were jealous of his wife. As for Wilhemina, where was she now, that poor, doubly deceived woman who had so much love to offer and yet had been twice denied? How much did she really understand that silent, impenetrable child who was at this very moment sitting on the pallet of the tiny cell next to the sacristy, rocking back and forth like an idiot, physically conscious but mentally completely withdrawn?

Was she an idiot? Was she a witch? Was she just one of those strange products of nature which man in his ignorance could never understand?

He remembered Klaus's words . . . 'She was lovely. She looked like an angel.'

Angel, devil, witch, idiot. What was this creature that denied all love yet loved a cat in the forest? How was she to be judged? Would any among this crowd of half-frightened sensation seekers really look for the truth?

If he had expected to have a few days in which to study her and reach some conclusion of his own, he now realized the futility of it. The child could never tell him anything and neither could Klaus nor Wilhemina, beyond that which they had already confessed. Was it enough to condemn her? The priest was unsure. If only someone could verify the child's origin. Was she really the daughter of the witch that was hanged in Sebastian's village? That would be proof enough to condemn her even if the cat could never be found.

Again he raised his hand for silence.

'I have decided to let you all be the judges. But first

we must have more proof. I want some of you to go to the forest to look for the cat. If you can find it, it must be brought here immediately, alive or dead. As for those among you who are neighbours of the man Sebastian, you will each be called upon in turn to either confirm or deny the story he has told, and I hope you will all remember that you will be under oath to speak truthfully. The rest of you can go back to your work until the trial shall be held. I want no more scandal or violence this day.'

The headman spoke with a few of the villagers who together went up to Klaus. 'You know where you last saw the child with the cat. You must take us to the place and help us look for it. Any objection?'

Klaus shook his head. He would have objected, except that he knew it was useless. And so he led them back to the place of Agnes's only happiness, replying to none but the most essential questions, torn with anxiety for his wife, not knowing what could have happened to her.

When would this nightmare, suffocating their whole existence, come to an end? Was it a nightmare or was it reality? Who and what was the child to whom he had given his daughter's name? Would they ever know and even if they found out, would it be too late to save them from destruction?

Twenty-two

While Klaus retraced his steps to the sunny forest glade in search of the cat, Wilhemina was already far away from there. She had no thoughts of what might be happening in the village that morning, intent only on finding a safe place for the cat and so preserve its life for Agnes's sake.

In her haste and fear she had hardly dared to examine it, seeing that it was still alive though only just. Half its life must have drained away overnight before the blood ceased to flow and it had limply allowed her to place it in the basket and cover it with the lid, hardly even opening its eyes. It neither moved nor made a sound as she hurried to the only place that was reasonably safe from prying eyes, the stream with the seven stones, and until she reached it she would not feel secure.

The sun was glinting brightly on the water beyond the yew trees' shade and the dish of curds which she had brought the evening before lay upturned on the middle stone, its contents vanished.

No one ever ventured into the grove of yew trees, which was always dark on the brightest day. It was such a silent, forbidding place, carpeted with creeping ivy from between whose luxuriant leaves toadstools sprang in profusion, that only faith in the woodland spirits and dire necessity made Wilhemina control her instinctive fear.

She crossed into the shadow, immediately aware of the chill of this place where the sun never reached, and set the basket down among some roots. Then, holding her

breath, she removed the lid and stared again at the
creature she had rescued, animal or witch she did not
know but as necessary to Agnes as the air she breathed.

So this miserable bundle of grubby fur was the cat!
She could not understand why her husband had been
frightened. Perhaps it was so close to death that all its
power had gone. Unconsciously, she shook her head,
wondering what kind of fear this creature could inspire.
It was so small and nearly weightless. Why had Agnes
loved it so? Why had Klaus and Josef feared it?

It stirred slightly, twitching its ears and half-opening
its eyes. There was an opacity in them that made her
think of Agnes. Eyes of death. Eyes of lifelessness. Was it
too late to save it? Had she only brought it here to see
it die?

She hurried back to the stream, rinsed out the bowl and filled it with water. Then gently she lifted the cat from the basket and laid it on the ground near the water. Its head came up with surprising swiftness and soon it was lapping with desperate thirst, half-raising itself, forgetting its weakness in its need. A second time Wilhemina filled the bowl, for soon she heard its tongue rasping against the dry base, and as she watched it satisfy its thirst with such anxiety, an involuntary smile softened her taut expression. This cat would live! A creature with such a thirst to satisfy would not let itself die so easily.

And now that she saw it closely and observed its movements, she could see that it was an animal like any other. Strange beasts which she had never seen were mentioned in the Bible but being strange did not make them evil. She saw the noose mark round its neck but, more than anything else, it reminded her of the time she had seen a man in the village with a performing bear. The huge creature wore an iron collar round its neck and she had noticed that the constant rubbing had worn its hair away. Perhaps this animal had at some time been a captive. Perhaps this was why it was tame.

All her fear was gone by now and she was convinced that there could be no evil in the child's association with the cat. If only Klaus could see the animal now! Surely he too would be convinced. She pondered taking it home with her, instead of keeping it here, but decided to stay by her original decision. She would tend the animal here, bring it food, cleanse its wounds if necessary, keep it safe for Agnes. A new hope filled her for she could never believe that the village people would condemn her little daughter, whose only sin was that she was different from everyone else.

The cat allowed her to examine its wounds, catching at her hands with its claws but not with evil intention, only in fear. She soothed it with gentle words and saw that the wounds might heal themselves. At least they no longer bled. The cat began to rub its head and jaw against her arm and a strange, soft sound swelled in its throat, as if it sang to itself with contentment. The tiredness in Wilhemina's heart fell away as she listened.

Just then she heard shouts and, looking up, saw a crowd of neighbours coming towards the stream, climbing the sloping meadow with officious eagerness. Had anyone seen her come here? Were they actually looking for her?

Hastily she thrust the cat into the basket again and covered it with the lid. She began digging at the soft mould with her hands, tossing it over the basket, dragging rotting branches and tendrils of ivy towards it too in an effort to disguise it. Would they see her among the trees if she hid behind a trunk and stayed very still? What would happen if they found her?

Now they were at the water's edge, where they halted. She could hear their words quite plainly and recognized them all. Three of them were women who had sometimes come to the stream with offerings. They were pointing towards the grove.

'There she is. She must be there. There's no other place she could hide in.'

Heart beating painfully, she pressed herself against the tree trunk, taking comfort from its hardness. Surely it would protect her from their sight, if only they would not dare to cross into the darkness. But they were as bold as she that day and within a moment she found herself surrounded by her neighbours who had trampled the toadstools and ivy underfoot, noisily confident. They discovered the basket, too, which she had hidden so hastily and one man kicked off the lid, revealing the crouching, startled cat within.

It hissed at them, sensing their animosity. The flattened

ears and savage expression in the sunken eyes gave a ferocious challenge to its appearance which caused them to draw back involuntarily, crossing themselves. Not one of them dared to touch it but Wilhemina hastily bent to replace the lid, not trusting them.

'Witch!' one of them spat in her face as she rose, tearing the shawl from her shoulders. They might all have set on her at that moment had not the men pulled them aside, one of them warning, 'Leave her alone if you don't want to be cursed.'

'Pick up that basket!' ordered another, giving her a rough push as if to prove that he was bolder and less superstitious than the rest.

Wilhemina stared at him uncomprehendingly. Could this be Erich who so often helped her husband with the harvest and who had several times supped at her table with his wife and children?

'Go on with you. Pick up that animal. You shouldn't have tried to hide it. It'll go badly with you for that.'

He pushed her again, nearly knocking her over, and as she did as she was bade she could understand why Klaus had been so frightened for them all.

Twenty-three

Wilhemina was taken to the public hall, which was more crowded than she had ever seen it. In vain she looked for Klaus among the bright-eyed, excited faces. She recognized the strange woman to whom she had given some fruit . . . was it only a few nights ago? And she looked about for Agnes, wondering what could have happened to her.

She was pushed into a corner, still holding the basket, and a ring of men formed round her, their backs towards her. People kept jostling up, glancing furtively into her face as if they had never seen it before. She caught sight of Josef, still accompanied by that rogue Sebastian, but he refused to look in her direction after once accidentally catching her eye.

Then she became aware of a particular gaze fixed upon her, that of a man who in spite of the crowd managed to keep himself aloof. There was something in his expression which held the frightened woman's attention. Why did he look at her so? Who was he? He was the only one there, as far as she could see, who seemed neither pleased nor excited by the events. His dark eyes expressed only bitterness and scorn, and some other stronger feeling which Wilhemina could not translate. Why did he watch her? What did he want?

Endlessly she stood there, crushed in the corner, her feet tangled in the straw that had been the strangers' beds. Her heart beat painfully fast. Her face was scarlet. Where was Klaus and where was Agnes? What would these people, who yesterday had been her neighbours, do?

Her eyes darted from face to face, looking for a sign of friendship or a glance of compassion, but most of their stares were directed at the basket in which the beast was held a prisoner and if they reached her, eyes were hastily turned away, whether from shame or fear she could not tell. And still that strange man looked at her. It seemed as though a secret battle waged within him.

Then the priest appeared, followed by a group of men with Klaus among them. He gave a cry when he recognized his wife in the corner but was not allowed to join her. The priest called for silence and when it was obtained he began to speak.

'Neighbours,' he cried. 'We are here today to judge some curious circumstances. No one here is, I believe, ignorant of the story that Josef and Sebastian have revealed but because fact and rumour have become so mixed the best thing I can do is try to set the details straight before we go any further.'

'Where's the child? We want to see the child.'

'No purpose can be gained by having her here,' replied the priest. 'She cannot speak and, since I've had her in my custody, I'm most firmly convinced that she's an idiot.'

He then went on to expound the facts as he had understood them from Josef and Sebastian and people were murmuring and arguing among themselves long before he had finished. Several times he had to call for silence but only really gained unanimous attention at the end of his discourse, when he summed up the vital points.

'Sebastian has told us that the woman was a witch and that the child was definitely acknowledged as her daughter, although her appearance was surrounded by mystery. He claims that this same child is the one we know as Agnes and that the cat she associates with is, through a magical and evil process, the incarnation of her dead mother, which the marks of the noose about its neck will prove. Whether Klaus's daughter was deliberately killed by witchcraft in order that this other child might some day take its place is, I think, too difficult to prove. But what must be proved or disproved here today is the truth of these men's words.'

Sebastian told his story again, embellished by details previously forgotten or not then imagined and when he had finished the mood of the crowd was definitely in his favour. Then it was Josef's turn to repeat once more what he had seen. He was a poor witness, but convincing by his very fearfulness. Klaus was called upon to speak but refused to say a word, neither confirming nor denying the story he had told the priest the night before. Someone threw a stone at him which hit him on the cheek, making his wife cry out with pain. And then it was Wilhemina's turn.

She was escorted towards the priest, the basket protectively in her arms, and people quickly made way for her, afraid that she might touch them. They stared at the basket with suspicious dread, as if all the evil in the world were contained therein, and utter silence filled the hall as she was told by the priest to remove the animal from its shelter and hold it up for all to see.

People gasped and crossed themselves, the priest included.

'See the marks of the noose!' shouted Sebastian above the varied exclamations of disgust and fear. 'As black as the witch herself, it is, and no one can deny it.'

'Why did you try to hide this animal?' the priest demanded, for he had been informed previously of all that had happened.

'I only wanted to save it for Agnes. It's a harmless

creature. There's no evil in it. It's only a cat that brought a few hours of happiness to a little girl.'

There was a howl of rage at her words.

'She's a witch too. Perhaps she murdered her own daughter, years ago.'

This was too much for Klaus.

'Savages!' he cried. 'You don't know what you're saying! You're all mad, mad,' and he began struggling towards his wife, held back by half a dozen men who took pleasure in his distress.

Suddenly, without knowing why or how or who it was, there was another man dragging at the arms of his captors, pulling and pushing them aside, making Klaus's battle his own, until within moments, in spite of the priest's shouts for order, a struggle ensued involving more than a dozen men. Fists and elbows and feet were flying, with blows badly aimed or not felt in the heat of the moment, and in the general confusion Klaus found himself free and face to face with his wife. She held the cat clutched to her chest, as if determined to protect it against all the world, careless of its reputation and her own, and the defiant expression which distorted all her features was directed as much against him as the accusers on every side.

'Wilhemina,' he managed to gasp; then, with some bewilderment, looked to the man who had helped him, who was still warding off the blows and kicks of those who would throw him out of the hall for his disorder. He was one of the strangers, the man he had listened to at the tavern! Nothing made sense that day. The struggle was going on right in front of the priest, who found himself obliged to push himself backwards in order not to be caught up in it.

'Throw him out! Get him out of here! What does he think he's doing?'

134

The tension that strained in every heart burst hysterically forth as everyone within reach threw himself on the stranger, shouting and screeching, wildly using fists and feet and more often than not kicking one of their own neighbours in the struggle. Klaus felt no compunction about staying out of the fight, not even realizing that he had unwittingly begun it with his cry of 'Savages!' and his attempt to reach his wife to protect her.

As Martin began to get the worst of it – he was almost on his knees but still resisting, butting with his head from which the bandage had been lost and where the previous wound was bleeding afresh more profusely than his nose – Klaus fearfully realized just how quickly the crowd would turn on him and his wife and the child. There would be no one to defend them except this stranger who must be mad for interfering and whom they were determined to silence even before he opened his mouth, by sheer battering if necessary, without even knowing why.

A movement beside him drew his attention back to Wilhemina who was carefully replacing the cat in the basket, even now remembering that she must preserve its life at all cost. She clutched the basket against her body, shielding it with her arms, and in spite of the crush all about her, people were able to shrink away, fearful of her touch. Klaus saw them and knew that just one spark was all that would be needed for these self-same cowards to fling themselves upon her and tear both her and the cat to pieces.

He looked round wildly, desperately. If only there were some escape from this madhouse without being seen! It was as if the whole universe had suddenly gone berserk in the little space of the public meeting hall, which before had heard only song and laughter and the mild admonishments of the headman or priest on special occasions, and here was this stranger, getting himself a beating for a cause that was not his own, the priest powerless to intervene in events that were no longer within his control!

Martin had given up defending himself and was being dragged towards the door, hands grasping him everywhere. He managed to halt his departure by jamming his foot against the doorpost and refusing to budge, at the same time shouting above the somewhat diminished noise, 'I have a right to speak. I demand to be heard. I want justice. Justice. You can't throw me out without first listening to me. Listen to me. That's all I ask. Listen to me. There can't be any justice until you've heard what I have to say.'

His strength, his courage, his determination to speak in spite of the brutal replies his words received – and even curiosity to know what he was so insistent on saying – at last moved his captors to reason. The noise abruptly abated and the priest took advantage of the breathless moment to demand, 'Bring that man here to me at once. Enough of this barbarism! Each man here has a right to speak and be heard.'

Just as he had been dragged towards the doorway, now he was equally pushed and pulled back across the hall to confront the priest, who was pale with emotion. Klaus looked at the grim, cut face of the stranger and momentarily saw himself. He had felt those pitiless, grasping hands only a short while since and knew only too well the sense of helplessness their grip inspired. He had had the sense not to struggle against them but this man had fought like an animal in a battle that was not his own. Why? Why? What had it to do with him?

The eyes of the priest and the stranger met and now the priest remembered who this man was, astonishment replacing anxiety as he recognized the trouble-maker. He had taken him to be a serious-minded, peaceful man and was almost ashamed that the figure he had instinctively respected should have received such rough treatment right in front of him.

'What do you know of all this?' he blustered, not knowing what to say and finding escape in self-righteous anger. 'If you know anything which will make the matter plainer, it's your duty to reveal it, which is what you should have done at the beginning instead of starting all this scandal.'

Martin chose to ignore the injustice of this remark, or perhaps he didn't feel it because, now that at last he had everyone's attention, his voice seemed to have failed him. Wilhemina, meanwhile, had untied her apron, offering it to him as a swab for the blood which trickled from his head and nose. She too had recognized him as the man with the troubled gaze who had watched her so intently.

Loud murmurings were beginning again as impatiently they waited to hear his words, careless of his discomfort, but they quieted again as, at last, breathing more steadily now, he said, 'I know about that other woman and I know about the child. I know whose child she is, if in truth that poor woman's child and this Agnes are one and the same. Every word that has been spoken here has been nothing but lies and conjectures from first to last.'

A new cry of outrage began at this, cut short by the priest's sharply raised hand as he said, 'Then let us hear what you know so that we may be the judges.'

Martin turned to face his attackers and the hall in general and a silence now fell which had never been achieved until that moment. There was something about his expression, beyond the marks of punishment, which inspired complete attention, something which very few there could have put into words but which most of them recognized: a visibly interior struggle, greater than what he had just endured physically, encompassing dread, shame, and even deeper emotions beyond the understanding of those who watched.

Not a soul spoke. All eyes were on the man, Martin, but of all who longed to hear his words only two hearts burned with fear and expectation, Klaus's and Wilhemina's.

Twenty-four

'She wasn't a witch,' began Martin. 'She was never a witch. She was just a poor woman no one understood. Old Hella was the only one who understood her. She gave her a home when her family died and cared for her when everyone else had turned their backs on her. It's true that she was a bit strange. She was lonely. She was never able to mix with other young people because they were all afraid of her. She was different, so dark when they were fair, defying the priest while they trembled under his gaze, seemingly so cold and hard while, in reality, she was the gentlest thing you could imagine.

'Sometimes she would fall down and go stiff and foam at the mouth. Old Hella said it was an illness. She had some plants that helped her when this happened. Once she said that when she was dead she didn't know who would look after her. She needed someone because she could choke to death if she fell down while she was alone.

'I knew old Hella well. She had helped to rear me, looking after me while my mother worked, and later, when my own wife was bearing children, she was there at every delivery, which is how we got to know Lina too. Lina! That was her name. Once Hella was dead no one ever called her by her name.'

He stopped, suddenly aware of the many eyes fixed steadily upon him. The hardest part was yet to come and he did not know if he would have the courage to tell it. Who would understand him? The priest would surely condemn him. His own neighbours would spurn and despise him. These two good-hearted strangers, Klaus and Wilhemina who watched him so intently now, had unwittingly been burdened with his sin. And yet, for the child's sake, the truth must be told, a truth he had hidden even from himself all these years until he had grown withdrawn and cynical – cynical because, having prided himself on his Christian honesty, in the moment of need he had been another Peter. He had shown cowardice when courage was needed. He had withheld the truth when the truth might have saved. He had failed in the most miserable way that any human being can fail.

'Well?' the priest reminded him, impatient of his silence. 'Have you, or have you not, something to tell us?'

As if no longer aware of the watching eyes, as if he were at long last confessing the secrets of his soul with only God to hear and judge him, Martin continued.

'Once I had a daughter, my eldest girl and second child. Her brother was nearly two when she was born. She was pretty and by the time she had left childhood behind most of the young men were in love with her. Perhaps I was at fault, perhaps my wife – both of us. We were proud of her, vain even, until one day we discovered that she was with child. The man she had hoped to marry had run off to the wars and later we learned that he had died.

'We kept her at home, pretending that grief had imprisoned her and thus none of the neighbours ever learned of her condition. By this time old Hella was dead and when the hour of birth came round the only person we could turn to in trust was Lina. She delivered the child but she could not keep my daughter from dying only a short while afterwards.

'The baby was too much of a problem for us. How to confess its existence? There was too much grief in our hearts for us to think clearly. In the end, only Lina offered us a solution. She would take the baby. She knew how to nurse it. Hella had taught her many things. As for what people might say – she laughed at their tongues. She was very lonely and had no hope of marriage. All she ever asked in return for her goodness and silence was that, if ever she were in need, we should befriend her. It was an easy promise to make.'

Here he uttered a short, bitter sound of self-mockery.

'At that moment we would have promised her the moon. We intended to keep the promise. I gave her part of my produce, vegetables, fruit, milk. She never went hungry but it was always in secret and no one ever knew. I heard the talk that went from mouth to mouth and in my heart I was sickened because I knew then how they would have spoken of my daughter. I knew, too, that I could never reveal the truth, for shame. It was easier to let Lina bear the brunt of their words for, after all, she didn't care. And such is a man's conscience that soon we ourselves came to forget the truth, to forget the great service Lina had done for us. It did not even seem that the baby was my grandchild.'

This last was spoken with a wondering tone, as if he himself could hardly believe even now of what a man was capable. Then the timbre of his voice changed, grew hard, self-condemning. Not a soul in that packed hall murmured. Wilhemina was seen to be weeping silently.

'The village fell on hard times. When it wasn't one sickness it was another. When it wasn't bandits it was soldiers. When the children didn't die the livestock did. The people were of one soul, resentful. They wanted a culprit, a victim, and there was one man who raised an accusing voice above the rest for reasons of his own. His son was dying and Lina refused to try to save him.'

'Lies, lies. She had cursed him,' broke in Sebastian but he was quickly silenced and, as for Martin, he went on as if unaware of the interruption.

'It was done in a matter of hours. Caught, tortured, condemned by a blood-lusting people that didn't even know what they were doing and yet could not be stopped. I was among them. I had gone – and God knows this is true – I had gone with the intention of saving her if I could, but when I felt the crowd's mood, when I saw how nothing would stop them, I was filled with fear and remained silent.

'Once she looked at me. Her tortured eyes clung to my face until I turned away. I was her only hope at that moment. Both of us knew it. The people might have listened to me, as they listened to Sebastian then. But at that moment I was more afraid than she was. All my guilt was before my eyes and I was incapable of stretching out a hand to succour her. Friendship? Where was friendship then? I was frightened. Frightened. I ran away. I didn't even think of the child. It was hers. It had nothing to do with me.

'I stopped my ears against her screams and while they dragged her off to the crossroads I was in my house, trying to find excuses for my behaviour. I remember finding several. It was my wife who said we must cut her free. I tried to stop her but she took no heed. She marched out of the house, obliging our eldest son to accompany her, and I had no choice but to follow.

'When we got there the people had gone away. They had left her hanging from a tree but she wasn't dead. It's not always easy to die. With my son's help I cut her loose and we stayed with her until she regained consciousness. My wife would have taken her home but I would have none of it. I told her to run away, to hide. She had time enough while the people's hot blood cooled. And then we left her leaning against the tree. I don't even remember seeing the child.

'Later, when I heard that her body had disappeared, I breathed freely again. She had got away. What did it matter if her strange disappearance was considered further evidence of witchcraft? She had already been condemned. Sometimes, at night, I would wonder what had become of her and the child. Now I believe I know.'

He made an impressive figure, his blood-matted head, swollen face and torn clothes starkly reminding them of his desperate fight for his right to be heard, and his eyes seared right through to the heart of every one of them as he went on, 'What happened in my own village so many years ago is happening here today. A child is being accused without any reasonable proof. Are you going to murder her, as that poor woman was murdered, on the strength of the same man's words?'

'She was a witch!' shouted Sebastian, alarmed at the way in which Martin's words had affected the crowd, for the first time seized by a sense of panic. The confession had surprised him more than anyone else and he forced conviction into his voice.

'What about the cat? That's real enough, as is the noose mark round its neck. Look at it, if no one wishes to believe my words, Look at it! The proof is there. It's not what I say, but what you can all see with your own eyes.'

There was a murmuring, but he no longer had the power to convince them. Martin dominated the scene and he disdained to answer, his very silence more eloquent than anything Sebastian might say now.

The priest said, 'I think Josef had better tell us what he knows about the cat, but the truth this time, un-embroidered by anyone's inventions.'

Josef seemed to have shrunk in size and it was not even

easy to find him for, as soon as he saw that Sebastian was discredited, he had tried to slink out of the hall. But he was stopped at the door and pushed back before the priest who gazed at him with stern, accusing eyes.

'Josef, remember you have sworn before God to speak truthfully. If you lied to us, your soul's in danger of hellfire.'

'It was Sebastian,' he burst out. 'He made me keep silent about the noose mark. I told him at the beginning what had happened. But all the rest is true. That child's bewitched. I know it.'

'What do you know about the cat, Josef? Just tell us.'

Miserably, and not without urging, he described that day in the forest when he found the cat in the trap and Agnes tending it, and then he had to admit that he had set the trap and for what purpose.

'If you had told the truth at the beginning you would never have been used by that rogue. As it is, you will have a lot to answer for,' the priest scolded him. 'And now,' he said, looking at Klaus and Wilhemina who at last had been allowed to get close to each other, 'I think Agnes must be brought here.'

He looked at Martin. 'Do you think you might be able to recognize her as your grandchild?'

'Perhaps. If there's anything of my daughter in her.'

'Then fetch her,' he said to the headman, giving him the key of her cell, 'and let us hope that this mystery may be solved for all time.'

Twenty-five

The previous night Agnes had been taken to the church and locked in the small room beside the sacristy. It was a cold, barren room, cell-like with its one narrow window high up near the ceiling and the pallet on the floor, grey with dust and age. There was a crucifix on the wall, above the pallet, and in one corner was a pile of old timbers and bits of broken furniture, for this little room really had no purpose except as a storehouse.

They had left her still unconscious, covered with the blanket that had been snatched with her from the cot, but she had awakened the next morning as if from a very deep sleep. When the priest went to examine her early in the day, he found her sitting cross-legged on the pallet, the blanket rucked about her, rocking back and forth and sometimes from side to side, her arms hugging her ribs, her face expressionless because of the lifelessness of her eyes.

The noise of the key in the lock, the priest's presence, even the light that streamed through the small window almost directly across her face had in no way altered her state or movements.

The priest had moved back and forth, watching to see if she observed his actions, but she was completely unaware of him. He spoke to her, calling her name several times quite sharply, but it was as if he were alone in the room. She was as animate as the stack of mouldering wood and her movements were as automatic as if only the very laws of equilibrium obliged her to fulfil them.

No wonder that he did not know how to judge her! No wonder that he had preferred to leave judgment in the hands of his parishioners, feeling that God would surely stir them to act rightly in this case. He had prayed beside her, raising his voice for both of them, and Agnes had gone on rocking, rocking, completely unaware of his existence.

How could anyone judge that state of utter darkness into which she had been plunged by the violent loss of the cat? Only the most agonizing depth of love and pain had wrenched those two sounds from her. Agnes was the cat. Agnes was herself, and Agnes had been mortally wounded by Klaus's senseless action in the forest.

She had lost consciousness because she could bear no more and when at last she woke it was only her body that awoke to begin its machine-like actions of every day. Her mind remained completely shut off from her physical self, the swaying, rocking motion being the most minimal expression of her instinctive need for self-comfort.

The priest had decided she was an idiot. It was the easiest explanation of the unexplainable and relieved him from any responsibility in the matter however the people should eventually judge her.

*

When they came for her that afternoon to take her to the public hall to be gazed upon in avid confusion she made no resistance and walked quite normally, if purely mechanical actions can be described as normal. They stood her before the priest, about whom most of the people were gathered, with Klaus, Wilhemina and Martin in the foreground and Sebastian nearby, brazenly intending to go on defending himself. The basket was on the ground. Neither sound nor movement came from within and

Wilhemina was secretly afraid that the creature might be dead.

She had refused to meet her husband's gaze, not knowing how he might react to her defiance of his will; ashamed for him, afraid for herself but, above all, determined to save the cat for Agnes, knowing that this was her only possible link between hope and utter desperation.

Very little had been spoken while they awaited the child's arrival. All of them were thinking of the terrible things she must have witnessed and suffered, and perhaps beginning to understand a little the reason for her withdrawal, the reason for her difference. Now it was easy for Wilhemina to understand many of the strange things about her and her heart ached with a longing to dispel the memory of terror that had been her only inheritance.

Klaus was painstakingly recalling the child's first days among them, trying to understand why she could never reach out to them in spite of the warmth they offered her. Even now it was beyond his understanding and each time his glance caught the basket and he thought of its contents he remembered how he had seen her in the forest, drenched with the light of happiness.

That black, devil's animal had converted her into a living, loving being in the secrecy of the forest, and in spite of his desire to see his wife contented, it still seemed to him a godless association.

As for Martin, both heart and mind were in a turmoil. His wife had died a few years earlier and he had lost his sons, together with his grandchildren, in the last attack of the bandits on the village. He was alone now, except for this child, should she be his granddaughter, and he was terribly afraid of having to look her in the face.

Did he want her to be his grandchild? Would he rather

she were a stranger and nothing to do with Lina's terrible fate? Would desire alone to recognize her cause him to find a non-existent likeness to that daughter whose features he could hardly recall, or would an instinctive dread of being confronted with his own guilt cause him to deny the smallest likeness that might actually exist?

If she were an idiot, as the priest proclaimed, surely it was his fault for having closed his heart against her. All that she had suffered was surely due to his cowardice, and it was hard to see the result of his treachery personified in a helpless, loveless child.

And now she stood among them, as understanding of the proceedings and the people about her as a cow might be, on sale in the marketplace, unaware and uninterested in its fate. A sob burst from Wilhemina as she caught the child and pressed her violently against her aching body, and Klaus's lips tightened with involuntary pain when Agnes made no reaction. Would it always be the same with him? Could he never forgive or understand her?

Gently, the priest separated the child from Wilhemina and turned her to face Martin. The man looked at her. The oval face, the thin nose, the pale lips in spite of the ruddy cheeks, the fair but tangled hair – they all made him think of his daughter as a child in a way that other, similar-looking children did not. Only her eyes were different. The same colour, it was true, but lacking that lively, laughing glow that even now caught at his heart with pain as he remembered.

'Well?' said the priest at length. 'Do you recognize her as your granddaughter? Can you honestly say whether or not she is any kin of yours?'

'Dear God, I wish I could,' he cried, 'but . . . It's so many years. She was hardly more than a baby, perhaps not even two years old. . . .'

'Look carefully. Is there nothing about her that recalls your daughter?'

'If my wife were here . . . Women are different. They recognize their own blood anywhere.'

Just then there was a shout from the main body of the people and a woman pushed herself forward.

'Shame on you, Martin, for not recognizing your own kin. The minute she walked into the hall my heart turned over as I looked at her, thinking it was your daughter.'

She was a plump, grey-haired grandmother who had staggered into the village with a couple of youngsters not her own who had lost their parents and families in the recent bloody sacking.

'I have listened to that Sebastian long enough. I always thought he was a rogue and never really believed that we did right when we hounded that poor woman to her death. And when you got up and spoke, at first I couldn't believe you, but I knew you'd never lie about anything so important. But when your own grandchild walks in here, looking so much like your daughter that I'd almost say it was her ghost, and you can't even recognize her – well, that's just too much for anyone to bear in silence. Look at her, man! Look at her well. If none of this had happened, if Lina hadn't died and she'd brought up the child in our village, your daughter's sin would have come out anyway, for she's the living proof of it. Well, God has punished her enough, I'd say, for the sins of her fathers.'

There was a general murmur of agreement in the hall. The unknown woman had more or less summed up their own feelings on the subject. Sebastian was discredited. Josef was scorned for his foolishness, although no one really expected anything better from him, and what little was left of their hysterical anxiety burst like an empty bubble, due to one man's determined resistance. A sense of relief had come secretly to each one of them.

'Martin,' said the priest. 'Do you accept that this child known as Agnes is indeed your grandchild?'

He nodded speechlessly.

'Yes or no? Speak!'

'Yes. She is my grandchild.'

'She's mine. She's mine,' moaned Wilhemina, looking at him with desperately beseeching eyes. 'You can't take her away from me.'

'There's time enough to talk about that,' interrupted Klaus. 'I want to know what redress I have against this Sebastian, who has brought so much grief and anxiety upon us.'

'Throw him out of the village! Stone him! Duck him in the river!'

The cries were vociferous and varied and, within a minute, the violence which might have been directed against the child accused of witchcraft was easily turned into another channel. Sebastian was pummelled and pushed and dragged out of the hall, helplessly begging for mercy. Josef was included in his disgrace but the villagers satisfied themselves with leaving him unconscious on the ground, face and body bruised, blood streaming from a gash in his temple.

Sebastian was flung bodily beyond the village limits and no one troubled to see if he was still alive when he did not rise. His clothes, what was left of them, were torn and bloody and a good many of his bones must have been broken.

Meanwhile, in the hall, Agnes still stood in front of that small body of people with the cat in the basket between them.

'Open the basket,' begged Wilhemina. 'Let her see the cat. I'm sure, when she sees it, she'll be better.'

Klaus shook his head. 'The cat is evil,' he insisted. 'I wish to God it had died.'

Martin was the one who knelt down at last and lifted the lid. The cat weakly raised its head, its sick yellow eyes staring from face to face. It recognized Agnes and mewed feebly, making a movement as if to rise but surrendering again to its weakness.

'Agnes. Look!' cried Wilhemina, taking her hand and drawing her closer to the basket, as if she could not see its contents from where she stood.

But Agnes did not even look down. Her unseeing eyes were aware of nothing.

Twenty-six

Klaus and Wilhemina took Agnes home. Martin accompanied them carrying the basket for the woman, who had her arms round the child, tightly embracing her all the way home. The villagers looked away shamefaced as the little group passed by, some of them involuntarily crossing themselves as their glance fell on the basket.

In a way the carrying home of Agnes was a repetition of the previous occasion, seven years earlier, except that then there had been hope in their hearts and now there was none. Wilhemina wept, Klaus bitterly forced himself to ignore her, Agnes was as indifferent now as then.

They halted with surprise at the open door and the disorder they glimpsed within, for neither of them knew how their home had been ransacked in their absence. Wilhemina gave a cry of dismay but even now she refused to let go of the child, watching while her husband put the furniture to rights, helped by Martin who left the basket beside her.

Agnes shook herself free of the protecting arms and went over to the pond, staring at the water which had always so attracted her. Wilhemina followed and stood beside her, wanting to touch her but holding back, desperately afraid that in spite of her efforts she had lost the child for good. She saw the wan reflection on the pond's smooth surface – a thin, fair child dressed in simple home-spun, the legs and arms bare, a ghost-like figure, less real in actuality than the reflection in the water.

Was it too late? Had she shut her heart and mind

against everything, including the cat? And if it were so, what future had she in the world she had utterly rejected as too cruel and unbearable in which to participate?

She allowed herself to be led away from the water, to be washed and fed and put to bed in due course. But she did not sleep. Several times Wilhemina looked at her and saw her with her eyes open, staring towards the ceiling. The flickering firelight and changing shadows had no effect on her. Not once did those eyes make the slightest movement.

Klaus said nothing while she tended the cat, making it comfortable in the basket beside the fireplace, feeding it with her own fingers because it seemed uninterested in feeding itself. He stared at the strange animal, containing his repulsion for his wife's sake, wondering how she could care for it with such devotion. It was as if the love Agnes rejected she gave to the cat.

Martin stayed to supper with them and Wilhemina tended the gash in his head, rebandaging it for him. At first they spoke in a general fashion, although none of them had much to say, their minds too full of what had happened that day and the doubts that had risen about the future. When Klaus at last broached the subject that was uppermost in their minds with the words, 'Well, Martin, what are your intentions with regard to this child?' Wilhemina broke in, 'She's ours. She's ours. He can't take her away.'

'I don't want to take her away from you. What would be the point? She doesn't know me. I don't know her. If she were normal, perhaps there might be some hope of our growing to love each other but – ' He looked from one to the other. 'You've sacrificed so much for her. I have no right to her love, assuming that anyone can gain it. I only wish there were some way in which I could repay you both for the trouble with which I burdened you.'

Klaus answered abruptly, 'We took her in good faith, with the intention of loving her like a daughter, but as you can see for yourself, it was impossible. Whether or not we like to admit it, she is a burden to us. A terrible burden and as the years go by that burden can only grow greater.'

He ignored his wife's unbelieving cry.

'It's easy for you to talk of having no right to her love and, with that excuse, leave her on our hands. I only wonder if you would talk the same way if she were as normal as any other child, pretty and gay and eager to please. Perhaps then you might consider taking her for consolation in your loneliness.'

'It wasn't my intention to – '

'I don't suppose any of your intentions were evil, not even now, and I daresay that as an honest man it will be a long time before you can forget your past sins, but that doesn't in any way help us to ease the burden of rearing an idiot child that isn't even our flesh and blood.'

'Klaus, Klaus,' moaned his wife. 'Please . . .'

'What would you have me do? If you want me to take her, I will. I'm prepared to pay for my sin. I only thought that your wife . . .'

'The child isn't leaving this house,' cried Wilhemina, standing up and confronting both men with wild, defiant eyes. 'She's not livestock, to be disposed of. She's not an idiot. She's a poor, poor creature that needs someone to love her. And I'm a poor creature that needs someone to love. Please, I appeal to you both. Leave her with me. Leave her with me.'

She fell on her knees, hands clenched together in an attitude of prayer, her whole body contorted by the agony of her desire. It was impossible for Klaus to resist her thus and abruptly he turned away from the sight of her with a grunt of exasperated defeat.

Who said that a man was master of his own house? He knew if he turned the child out Wilhemina would never forgive him and, resigned though he was to the bitterness of life, he could not live with her hatred for the rest of his days.

So it was decided and a few days later Martin went away as he had come, among the straggle of strangers returning to what might be left of their homes.

*

Meanwhile, Agnes showed no change of attitude. Never had Wilhemina known her in such a state and in spite of all she had gone through with her she was aware of a new fear. Before, there had always been hope. She had been contented in her introverted fashion, playing with stones and leaves, wandering about the fields and forest, and when she had found the cat, the change for the better had begun. Wilhemina had seen true happiness in her eyes. She had come alive.

But now she did nothing but allow herself to be led from the bed to the table, from the table to the garden where she sat unmoving in the sun or the shade until Wilhemina came to take her in at the end of the day. Wherever she was, Wilhemina left the cat beside her. It still moved very little and spent most of the time sleeping. Now and again it looked at Agnes and mewed softly but the child neither saw nor heard it.

Klaus watched his wife tend the child and the cat, and his hardness melted. Even he began to feel a certain pity for Agnes who, no longer the elusive, intangible shadow but an ever-present darkness in their lives, at last appeared to him as a child in need. She seemed smaller, more dependent, and whenever he recalled that moment when he had seen her in all her happiness, which he had destroyed, he cursed himself and the day that he had allowed his fear to rule him.

He, too, had to admit that the cat was no more than a cat and he could no longer remember clearly why it had seemed so evil to him. Sometimes he would stare down at it for several minutes, pleased to see that a shine was beginning to come to its coat again and that the wounds were healing well, if only because as a good husbandman the sight of a sick, unhealthy animal annoyed him.

One afternoon, when Agnes was sitting close to the pond, which was where Wilhemina usually left her because it had always been her favourite place, the cat suddenly decided it felt well enough to explore. Wilhemina was sitting nearby, mending her husband's shirt, and the cat was in the basket as usual. It had been pulling with its paws at the frayed edges, the warm sun filling it with a sense of well-being and playfulness.

It slid out of the basket and began rolling in the grass, rubbing its head on the ground, stretching its legs and, when it caught sight of its waving tail, grabbing at it with both teeth and claws. Wilhemina smiled at its antics then suddenly caught her breath as she saw Agnes unexpectedly turn her head and focus her gaze on the cat.

'Dear God,' she whispered to herself, 'don't let it stop playing now,' and all the time the cat squirmed and rolled, basking in the sun, Agnes's eyes upon it, Wilhemina prayed unceasingly that the longed-for miracle would occur.

Agnes did not move but her eyes did. They followed the cat's every action and the watching woman's heart leaped and burned with excitement just to see the difference in her expression when her eyes came alive. If only Klaus could have been there! He deserved to share this moment of hope, if only for his patience in spite of his disbelief. He was in the stable, tending the cows, but she dared not call him for fear of destroying the magic of that moment.

The cat suddenly sat up and looked at Agnes. It stood up, tail high, ears pricked, and then it unhurriedly went towards her, rubbing its head against the still arm, bit by bit caressing its whole body against her, tail quivering, eyes half-closed with pleasure. Then it turned and looked at her, its yellow eyes questioning as it uttered a tiny mew. It placed one paw on the child's lap and in a moment had its whole body there, while the head nuzzled and rubbed against her chest and its tail twitched under her nose.

She had to draw her head back because of the tickling tail and as she did so a hand came up to touch the demanding black creature that wanted her caresses. Slowly, as if uncertain or as if remembering a long forgotten but accustomed action, she drew her fingers softly along its back, brought them down behind its ears and rubbed them under its chin. The cat squirmed with delight and pushed itself closer and, as she rubbed and rubbed, she felt the soft vibrations of contentment in its throat which grew with each passing moment into a crescendo of pleasure, till the song, which she had known before, burst out of it.

And then Agnes hugged the animal to her, rocking back and forth in her delight, feeling its music against her breast, feeling it seep into her empty heart. Tears ran down her cheeks as she opened her mouth in a silent cry of joy, rubbing her face against the warm black body that filled her with love, and then she caught sight of Wilhemina watching her.

For a moment she was startled and the woman's heart automatically shrank with dread. Oh God, why had Agnes seen her in that moment? Would everything be destroyed once more? She saw the child rise to her feet, holding the cat against her breast, and come towards her, wet-faced, her expression a mixture of wonder and uncertainty.

Wilhemina was suddenly aware that Klaus had come out of the stable and was walking towards them. She was torn between the two. Would his presence kill once again whatever it was that had suddenly possessed her? Could he not see that something wonderful might be about to happen? Could he not stay his pace for just a few moments more?

These agonized thoughts rushed through her mind in seconds but then Agnes was in front of her, kneeling down and pushing the cat towards her. Her mouth opened as if to speak. Several times she tried to get out the word, or words she wanted to communicate. Wilhemina did not know it but her own mouth was open in exactly the same way, feeling what Agnes felt, longing for her to speak.

And at last – incredibly, miraculously – sound came.

'Agnes. Agnes,' she said.

Wilhemina flung her arms round the child, crushing both her and the cat against her, sobbing with joy. She felt her husband's hand on her shoulder and released the child to look up at him.

'Did you hear what she said? Did you hear her?' she cried.

He nodded, then transferred his gaze to Agnes who was once again rubbing her face against the cat, listening to its song. He took her chin in his grasp and gently turned her head upwards so that she must see him, and his rough thumb stroked her cheek.

She made a small movement with the cat, as if showing him the creature for the first time, and he nodded, removing his hand from her chin to caress the cat because it seemed to be what she wanted. She was watching him. She was looking at him. She was allowing him to share in her happiness and for the first time he felt a warmth in his heart towards her.

'Agnes,' he said, and again, 'Agnes,' as if at long last he was recognizing her. 'One day you will be our Agnes, God willing.'